Praise for *Playing with Fire*

"One of the best and most original thrillers of the year."
                    —*The Provi...*

"[A] novel brin... ...ry description, ...

"Will make ... everything to immerse themselves in ... ...pulsive dual narrative."
                    —*Los Angeles Times*

"Masterful . . . Clear your schedule for this one—you won't want to put it down until you're finished."
                    —*Kirkus Reviews*

"Haunting . . . Accurate historical details about an Italy on the brink of terrible war raise this story well above that of an ordinary thriller."
                    —*BookPage*

By Tess Gerritsen

Playing
with
Fire

A NOVEL

TESS GERRITSEN

BALLANTINE BOOKS • NEW YORK

Playing with Fire is a work of fiction. Names, characters, places, and incidents are the products of the author's imagination or are used fictitiously. Any resemblance to actual events, locales, or persons, living or dead, is entirely coincidental.

2016 Ballantine Books Export Edition

Copyright © 2015 by Tess Gerritsen
Excerpt from *The Strange Girl* by Tess Gerritsen copyright © 2016 by Tess Gerritsen

Published in the United States by Ballantine Books, an imprint of Random House, a division of Penguin Random House LLC, New York.

BALLANTINE and the HOUSE colophon are registered trademarks of Penguin Random House LLC.

Originally published in hardcover in the United States by Ballantine Books, an imprint of Random House, a division of Penguin Random House LLC, in 2007.

This book contains an excerpt from *The Strange Girl* by Tess Gerritsen. This excerpt has been set for this edition only and may not reflect the final content of the forthcoming edition.

ISBN 978-0-812-99930-3
ebook ISBN 978-1-101-88435-5

Cover design: Scott Biel
Cover image: Matteo Colombo/Moment/Getty Images; (woman) © Ilina Simeonova/Trevillion Images

Printed in the United States of America

randomhousebooks.com

9 8 7 6 5 4 3 2 1

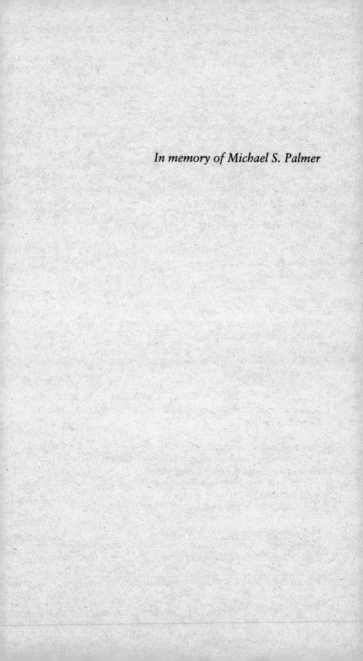

In memory of Michael S. Palmer

Playing with
with
Fire

Julia ❧

1

From the doorway I can already smell the scent of old books, a perfume of crumbling pages and time-worn leather. The other antiques stores that I've passed on this cobblestoned alley have their air conditioners running and their doors closed against the heat, but this shop's door is propped open, as if inviting me to enter. It's my last afternoon in Rome, my last chance to pick up a souvenir of my visit. Already I've bought a silk tie for Rob and an extravagantly ruffled dress for our three-year-old daughter, Lily, but I haven't found anything for myself. In the window of this antiques shop, I see exactly what I want.

I step into gloom so thick that my eyes need a moment to adjust. Outside it's sweltering, but in here it's strangely cool, as though I've entered a cave where neither heat nor light can penetrate. Slowly, shapes take form in the shadows and I see book-crammed shelves, old steamer trunks, and in the corner a medieval suit of tarnished armor. On the walls hang oil paintings, all of them garish and ugly and adorned with yellowed price tags. I don't notice that the proprietor is standing in the alcove, so I'm startled when he suddenly calls out to me in Italian. I turn and see a little gnome of a man with eyebrows like snowy caterpillars.

"I'm sorry," I answer. *"Non parlo Italiano."*

"Violino?" He points to the violin case that I have strapped to my back. It's far too valuable an instrument to leave in my hotel room and I always keep it with me while traveling. *"Musicista?"* he asks and plays air fiddle, his right arm sawing back and forth with a phantom bow.

"Yes, I'm a musician. From America. I performed this morning, at the festival." Though he nods politely, I don't think he actually understands me. I point to the item I spotted in his display window. "Could I see that book? *Libro. Musica.*"

He reaches into the window display for the book of music and hands it to me. I know it's old, by the way the edges of the paper crumble at my touch. The edition is Italian, and on its cover is the word *Gipsy* and an image of a shaggy-haired man playing the violin. I open it to the first tune, which is written in a minor key. The piece is unfamiliar, a plaintive melody that my fingers are already itching to play. Yes, this is what I'm always on the hunt for, old music that's been forgotten and deserves to be rediscovered.

As I flip through the other tunes, a loose page falls out and flutters to the floor. Not part of the book, it is a sheet of manuscript paper, its staves thick with musical notes jotted in pencil. The composition's title is handwritten in elegantly swooping letters.

Incendio, composed by L. Todesco.

As I read the music, I can hear the notes in my head and within a few measures, I know this waltz is beautiful. It starts as a simple melody in E minor. But at measure sixteen, the music grows more complex. By measure sixty, notes start to pile on notes and there are jarring accidentals. I flip to the other side and every measure is dense with pencil marks. A lightning-quick string of arpeggios launches the melody into a frantic maelstrom of notes that make the hairs suddenly rise on my arms.

I must have this music.

"Quanto costa?" I ask. "For this page and for the book as well?"

The proprietor watches me with a canny gleam in his eyes. *"Cento."* He pulls out a pen and writes the number on his palm.

"A hundred euros? You can't be serious."

"E' vecchio. Old."

"It's not *that* old."

His shrug tells me I can take it or leave it. He's already seen the hunger in my eyes; he knows he can charge me an outrageous price for this crumbling volume of Gypsy tunes and I'll pay it. Music is my only extravagance. I have no interest in jewelry or designer clothes and shoes; the only accessory I truly value is the hundred-year-old violin now strapped to my back.

He hands me a receipt for my purchase and I walk out of the shop, into afternoon heat that's as cloying as syrup. How odd that I felt so cold inside.

I look back at the building, but I don't see any air conditioner, just closed windows and twin gargoyles perched above the pediment. A shard of sunlight bounces back at me, reflected from the brass Medusa-head knocker. The door is now closed, but through the dusty window I glimpse the proprietor looking at me, just before he drops the shade and vanishes from sight.

My husband, Rob, is thrilled with the new tie I bought him in Rome. He stands at our bedroom mirror, expertly looping lustrous silk around his neck. "This is just the thing I need to jazz up a boring meeting," he says. "Maybe these colors will keep them all awake when I start going over the numbers." At thirty-eight, he's as lean and fit as the day we married, although the last ten years have added streaks of silver to his temples. In his starched white shirt and gold cuff links, my Boston-bred husband looks exactly like the meticulous accountant he is. He's all about numbers: profits and losses, assets and debts. He sees the world in mathematical terms, and even the way he moves has a precise geometry to it, his tie swinging an arc, crisscrossing into a perfect knot. How different we are! The only numbers I care about are symphony and opus numbers and the time signatures on my music. Rob tells everyone that's why he was attracted to me, because unlike him, I'm an artist and air creature who dances in the sunshine. I used to worry that our differences would tear us apart, that Rob, who keeps his feet so firmly planted on the ground, would grow weary of keeping his air-creature wife from floating away into the clouds. But ten years later, here we are, still in love.

He smiles at me in the mirror as he tightens the knot at his throat. "You were awake awfully early this morning, Julia."

"I'm still on Rome time. It's already twelve noon there. That's the upside of jet lag. Just think of all the things I'll get done today."

"I predict you'll be ready to collapse by lunchtime. You want me to drive Lily to day care?"

"No, I want to keep her home today. I feel guilty about being away from her all week."

"You shouldn't. Your aunt Val swooped in and took care of everything, the way she always does."

"Well, I missed her like crazy and I want to spend every minute with her today."

He turns to show me his new tie, perfectly centered on his collar. "What's on the agenda?"

"It's so hot, I think we'll go to the pool. Maybe drop into the library and choose some new books."

"Sounds like a plan." He bends to kiss me, and his clean-shaven face smells tart with citrus. "I hate it when you're gone, babe," he murmurs. "Maybe next time, I'll take the week off and we'll go together. Wouldn't that be a lot more—"

"Mommy, look! Look how pretty!" Our three-year-old daughter, Lily, dances into the bedroom and swirls around in the new dress I brought her from Rome, the dress that she tried on last night and now refuses to take off. Without warning she launches herself like a missile into my arms and we both tumble onto the bed, laughing. There is nothing so sweet as the smell of my own child, and I want to inhale every molecule of her, absorb her back into my own body so we can become one again. As I hug the giggling tangle of blond hair and lavender ruffles, Rob drops onto the bed, too, and wraps us both in his arms.

"Here are the two most beautiful girls in the world," he declares. "And they're mine, all mine!"

"Daddy, stay home," Lily orders.

"Wish I could, sweetie." Rob plants a noisy kiss on Lily's head and reluctantly gets back to his feet. "Daddy has to go to work, but aren't you a lucky girl? You get to spend *all day* with Mommy."

"Let's go put on our bathing suits," I tell Lily. "We're going to have a wonderful time, just you and me."

And we do have a wonderful time. We splash in the community pool. We eat cheese pizza and ice cream for lunch and go to the library, where Lily chooses two new picture books featuring donkeys, her favorite animal. But when we get home at three that afternoon, I'm almost comatose from exhaustion. As Rob predicted, jet lag has caught up with me and there's nothing I want to do more than to crawl into bed and go to sleep.

Unfortunately, Lily's wide awake and she's dragged the box of her old baby clothes out onto the patio, where our cat, Juniper, is snoozing. Lily loves dressing up Juniper and already she's tied a bonnet around his head and is working one of his front paws into a sleeve. Our sweet old cat endures it as he always does, indifferent to the indignities of lace and ruffles.

While Juniper gets his fashion makeover, I bring my violin and music stand onto the patio and open the book of Gypsy tunes. Once again, the loose sheet of music slips out, landing faceup at my feet. *Incendio*.

I haven't looked at this music since the day I bought it in Rome. Now, as I clip the page to the stand, I think of that gloomy antiques shop, and the proprietor, lurking like some cave creature in the alcove. Goose bumps suddenly stipple my skin, as if the chill of the shop still clings to this music.

I pick up my violin and begin to play.

On this humid afternoon, my instrument sounds deeper, richer than ever, the tone mellow and warm. The first thirty-two bars of the waltz are as beautiful as I'd imagined, a lament in a mournful baritone. But at measure forty, the notes accelerate. The melody twists and turns, jarred by accidentals, and soars into seventh position on the E string. Sweat breaks out on my face as I struggle to stay in tune and maintain the tempo. I feel as if my bow takes off on its own, that it's moving as though bewitched and I'm just struggling to hang on to it. Oh, what glorious music this is! What a performance piece, if I can master it. The notes skitter up the scale. Suddenly I lose all control and everything goes off-pitch, my left hand cramping as the music builds to a frenzy.

A small hand grasps my leg. Something warm and wet smears my skin.

I stop playing and look down. Lily stares up at me, her eyes as clear as turquoise water. Even as I jump up in dismay and wrench the garden tool from her bloody hand, not a ripple disturbs her calm blue eyes. Her bare feet have tracked footprints across the patio flagstones. With growing horror, I follow those footprints back to the source of the blood.

That's when I start screaming.

2

Rob helps me wash the cat's blood from the patio. Poor old Juniper is now wrapped in a black trash bag, awaiting burial. We've dug the hole for his grave in the far corner of the yard, behind the lilac bush, so I will not have to look at it whenever I come into the garden. Juniper was eighteen years old and almost blind, a gentle companion who deserves a better eternity than a trash bag, but I was too shaken to come up with any alternative.

"I'm sure it was just an accident," Rob insists. He tosses the dirty sponge into the bucket and the water magically turns a nauseating shade of pink. "Lily must have tripped and fallen on him. Thank God she didn't land with the sharp end up, or she could have put out her eye. Or worse."

"I wrapped him in the trash bag. I saw his body, and it wasn't just a single stab wound. How do you trip and fall *three times*?"

He ignores my question. Instead, he picks up the murder weapon, a dandelion fork tipped with prongs, and asks, "How did she get her hands on this thing, anyway?"

"I was out here weeding last week. I must have forgotten to put it back in the tool shed." There's still blood on the prongs and I turn away. "Rob, doesn't it bother you how she's reacting to all this? She stabbed Juniper and a few minutes later, she asked for juice. That's what freaks me out, how perfectly calm she is about what she did."

"She's too young to understand. A three-year-old doesn't know what death means."

"She must have known she was hurting him. He must have made *some* kind of sound."

"Didn't you hear it?"

"I was playing the violin, right here. Lily and Juniper were at that end of the patio. They seemed perfectly fine together. Until . . ."

"Maybe he scratched her. Maybe he did something to provoke her."

"Go upstairs and take a look at her arms. She doesn't have a single mark on her. And you know how sweet that cat was. You could yank on his fur, step on his tail, and he'd never scratch you. I've had him since he was just a kitten, and for him to die this way . . ." My voice cracks and I sink into a patio chair as it all washes over me, a tidal wave of grief and exhaustion. And guilt, because I couldn't protect my old friend, even as he bled to death only twenty feet away. Rob awkwardly pats my shoulder, not knowing how to comfort me. My logical, mathematical husband is helpless when it comes to dealing with a woman's tears.

"Hey. Hey, babe," he murmurs. "What if we got a new kitten?"

"You can't be serious. After what she did to Juniper?"

"Okay, that was a stupid idea. But please, Julia, don't blame her. I bet she misses him just as much as we do. She just doesn't understand what happened."

"Mommy?" Lily cries out from her bedroom, where I've put her down for her nap. *"Mommy!"*

Though I'm the one she's calling for, it's Rob who lifts her out of her bed, Rob who cradles her in his lap as he sits in the same rocking chair where I once nursed her. As I watch them, I think of the nights when she was still an infant and I rocked her in that chair, hour after hour, her velvety cheek snuggled against my breast. Magical, sleep-deprived nights when it was just Lily and me. I'd stare into her eyes and whisper: "Please remember this. Always remember how much Mommy loves you."

"Kitty gone away," Lily sobs into Rob's shoulder.

"Yes, darling," Rob murmurs. "Kitty's gone to heaven."

"Do you think that's normal behavior for a three-year-old?" I ask the pediatrician a week later, at Lily's well-baby visit. Dr. Cherry is examining Lily's belly, eliciting her giggles as he presses on her abdomen, and he doesn't immediately answer my question. He seems to genuinely like children and Lily responds by being her charming best. Obediently she turns her head so he can look at her eardrums, opens her mouth wide as he inserts the tongue depressor. My lovely daughter already knows how to enchant every stranger she meets.

He straightens and looks at me. "Aggressive behavior isn't necessarily something to worry about. At this age, children get easily frustrated because they can't fully express themselves. And you said she's still using mostly three- and four-word sentences."

"Is that something I should worry about? That she's not talking as much as other kids?"

"No, no. Developmental milestones aren't set in concrete. There's a great deal of variability among children, and Lily's progressing as expected in every other way. Her height and weight, her motor skills, are all perfectly normal." He sits her up on the side of the exam table and gives her a big smile. "And what a good little girl you are! I wish all my patients were so cooperative. You can see how focused she is. How closely she pays attention."

"But after what happened to our cat, does that mean she might do something even worse when she's . . ." I pause, realizing that Lily is watching me and listening to everything I say.

"Mrs. Ansdell," he says quietly, "why don't you take Lily into our playroom? You and I should discuss this alone, in my office."

Of course, he's right. My clever, attentive daughter almost certainly understands more than I realize. I take her from the exam room and lead her into the patients' play area, as he requests. The room has toys scattered everywhere, bright plastic things with no sharp edges, no little parts that can be swallowed by indiscriminating mouths. Kneeling on the floor is a boy about her age, making engine noises as he pushes a red dump truck across the carpet. I set Lily down and she heads straight to a child-size table with plastic teacups and a teapot. She picks up the pot and pours invisible tea. How does she know to do that? I've never thrown a tea party, yet here's my daughter, performing stereotypical girl behavior while the boy *zoom-zooms* with his truck.

Dr. Cherry is sitting behind his desk when I step into his office. Through the viewing window, we can watch the two children in the next room; on their side is a one-way mirror, so they cannot see us. They play in parallel, ignoring each other in their separate boy and girl worlds.

"I think you're reading too much into this incident," he says.

"She's only three and she's killed our family pet."

"Was there any warning before this happened? Any sign that she was going to hurt him?"

"None at all. I've had Juniper since before I got married, so Lily's known him all her life. She was always perfectly gentle with him."

"What might have set off this attack? Was she angry? Was she frustrated by something?"

"No, she looked perfectly content. They were so peaceful together, I let them play while I practiced my violin."

He considers this last detail. "I assume that takes a lot of concentration, playing the violin."

"I was trying out a new piece of music. So, yes, I was focused."

"Maybe that explains it. You were busy doing something else, and she wanted to get your attention."

"By stabbing our cat?" I give a laugh of disbelief. "That's a drastic way of going about it." I look through the viewing window at my golden-haired daughter, seated so prettily at her imaginary tea party. I don't want to bring up the next possibility, but I have to ask him. "There was an article I read online, about children who hurt animals. It's supposed to be a very bad sign. It could mean the child has serious emotional issues."

"Trust me, Mrs. Ansdell," he says with a benign smile. "Lily is not going to grow up to be a serial killer. Now if she *repeatedly* hurt animals, or if there's a history of violence in the family, then I might be more concerned."

I say nothing; my silence makes him frown at me.

"Is there something you wanted to share?" he asks quietly.

I take a deep breath. "There *is* a history in the family. Of mental illness."

"On your husband's side or on yours?"

"Mine."

"I don't recall seeing anything about that in Lily's medical records."

"Because I never mentioned it. I didn't think something like that could run in families."

"Something like what?"

I take my time answering, because while I want to be truthful, I don't want to tell him more than I need to. More than I'm comfortable with. I look through the playroom window at my beautiful daughter. "It happened soon after my brother was born. I was only two years old at the time, so I don't remember anything about it. I learned the details years later from my aunt. I'm told my mother had some sort of mental breakdown. She had to be sent to an institution because they felt she was a danger to others."

"The timing of her breakdown makes it sound like a case of postpartum depression or psychosis."

"Yes, that's the diagnosis I heard. She was evaluated by several psychiatrists and they concluded she wasn't mentally competent and couldn't be held responsible for what happened."

"What did happen?"

"My brother—my baby brother—" My voice softens to a whisper. "She dropped him and he died. They said she was delusional at the time. Hearing voices."

"I'm sorry. That must have been a painful time for your family."

"I can't imagine how terrible it was for my father, losing a child. Having my mother sent away."

"You said your mother went to an institution. Did she ever recover?"

"No. She died there two years later, from a ruptured appendix. I never really knew her, but now I can't stop thinking about her. And I wonder if Lily—if what she did to our cat . . ."

Now he understands what I'm afraid of. Sighing, he takes off his glasses. "I assure you, there's no connection. The genetics of violence isn't as simple as Lily inheriting your blue eyes and blond hair. I know of only a few documented cases where it's clearly familial. For example, there's a family in the Netherlands where almost every male relative has been incarcerated. And we know that boys born with extra Y chromosomes are more likely to commit crimes."

"Is there an equivalent in girls?"

"Girls can be sociopaths, of course. But is that genetic?" He shakes his head. "I don't think the data supports it."

The data. He sounds like Rob, who's always citing numbers and statistics. These men have such faith in their numbers. They refer to scientific studies and quote the latest research. Why doesn't that reassure me?

"Relax, Mrs. Ansdell." Dr. Cherry reaches across the desk and pats my hand. "At three years old, your daughter is perfectly normal. She's engaging and affectionate and you said she's never done anything like this before. You have nothing to worry about."

Lily has fallen asleep in her car seat by the time I pull into my aunt Val's driveway. It's her usual naptime and she sleeps so deeply that she doesn't stir as I lift her out of the seat. Even in her sleep she clutches Donkey, who goes everywhere with her and is looking rather disgusting lately, frayed and drool-stained and probably teeming with bacteria. Poor old Donkey's been patched and repatched so many times that he's turned into a Frankenstein animal, zigzagged with my amateurish seams. Already I can see another new rip starting in the fabric, where his stuffing is starting to poke through.

"Oh, look how adorable she is," coos Val as I carry Lily into her house. "Just like a little angel."

"Can I put her on your bed?"

"Of course. Just leave the door open so we can hear if she wakes up."

I carry Lily into Val's bedroom and gently set her down on the duvet. For a moment I watch her, enchanted as I always am by the sight of my slumbering daughter. Leaning close, I breathe in her scent and feel the heat rising from her pink, flushed cheeks. She sighs and murmurs "Mommy" in her sleep, a word that always makes me smile. A word I'd ached to hear during the heartbreaking years when I repeatedly tried and failed to get pregnant.

"My baby," I whisper.

When I return to the living room, Val asks: "So what did Dr. Cherry say about her?"

"He says there's nothing to worry about."

"Isn't that what I told you? Kids and pets don't always mix well. You don't remember this, but when you were two, you kept pestering my old dog. When he finally gave you a nip, you slapped him right back. I'm thinking that's what happened between Lily and Juniper. Sometimes children react without thinking. Without understanding the consequences."

I look out the window at Val's garden, a little Eden crammed with tomato plants and lush herbs and cucumber vines scrambling up the trellis. My late father liked to garden, too. He liked to cook and recite poetry and sing off-key, just like his sister, Val. They even look alike in their childhood photos, both of them skinny and tanned, with matching boyish haircuts. There are so many photos of my dad displayed in Val's house that every visit here gives me a sad tug on my heart. On the wall facing me are pictures of my dad at ten years old with his fishing rod. At twelve with his ham radio set. At eighteen, in his high school graduation robe. Always he wears the same earnest, open smile.

And on the bookshelf is the photo of him and my mother, taken on the day they brought me home as a newborn. It's the sole image of my mother that Val allows in her house. She tolerates it only because I appear in it, too.

I stand to examine the faces in the photo. "I look just like her. I never realized how much."

"Yes, you do look like her, and what a beauty she was. Whenever Camilla walked into the room, heads would turn. Your dad got one eyeful, and fell head over heels in love. My poor brother never had a chance."

"Did you hate her all that much?"

"Hate her?" Val thinks about this. "No, I wouldn't say that. Certainly, not at first. Like everyone else who ever met her, I was completely sucked in by Camilla's charm. I've never met any other woman who had it all, the way she did. Beauty, brains, talent. And oh, what a sense of style."

I give a regretful laugh. "*That* I certainly didn't inherit."

"Oh, honey. You inherited the best of both your parents. You got Camilla's looks and musical talent and you got your dad's generous heart. You were the best thing that ever happened to Mike. I'm just sorry he had to fall in love with *her* first, before you could come into the world. But hell, everyone else fell in love with her. She had that way of sucking you right into her force field."

I think of my daughter and how easily she enchanted Dr. Cherry. At three years old, she already knows how to charm everyone she meets. That's a gift I never had, but Lily was born with it.

I set my parents' photo back on the shelf and turn to Val. "What really happened to my brother?"

My question makes her stiffen and she looks away; clearly it's something she doesn't want to talk about. I've always known there was something more to the story, something far darker and more disturbing than I've been told, and I've avoided pressing the matter. Until now.

"Val?" I ask.

"You know what happened," she says. "I told you as soon as I felt you were old enough to understand."

"But you didn't tell me the details."

"Nobody wants to hear the details."

"Now I need to." I glance toward the bedroom where my daughter, my darling daughter, is sleeping. "I need to know if Lily's anything like her."

"Stop, Julia. You are going down the wrong path if you think Lily bears *any* resemblance to Camilla."

"All these years, I've heard only bits and pieces about what happened to my brother. But I always sensed there was more to the story, things you didn't want to say."

"The whole story won't make it any easier to understand. Even thirty years later, I still don't understand why she did it."

"What exactly *did* she do?"

Val considers the question for a moment. "After it happened—when it finally went to court—the psychiatrists called it postpartum depression. That's what your father believed, too. It's what he *wanted* to believe, and he was so relieved when they didn't send her to prison. Fortunately for her, they sent her to that hospital instead."

"Where they let her die of appendicitis. That doesn't sound so fortunate to me."

Val is still not looking at me. The silence grows so thick between us that it will turn solid if I don't cut through it now. "What aren't you telling me?" I ask quietly.

"I'm sorry, Julia. You're right, I haven't been entirely honest. Not about that, at least."

"About what?"

"How your mother died."

"I thought it was a ruptured appendix. That's what you and Dad always said, that it happened two years after she was sent there."

"It *was* two years later, but it wasn't from a ruptured appendix." Val sighs. "I didn't want to tell you this, but you say you want the truth. Your mother died from an ectopic pregnancy."

"A *pregnancy*? But she was a prisoner in a mental ward."

"Exactly. Camilla never named the father, and we never found out who he was. After she died, when they cleaned her room, they found all sorts of contraband. Liquor, expensive jewelry, makeup. I have no doubt she was trading sex for favors, and doing it willingly, always the master manipulator."

"She was still a victim. She had a psychiatric illness."

"Yes, that's what the psychiatrists said in court. But I'm telling you, Camilla wasn't depressed and she wasn't psychotic. She was *bored*. And resentful. And fed up with your baby brother, who was colicky and crying all the time. She always wanted to be the center of attention and she was accustomed to having men trip over each other to make her happy. Camilla was the golden girl who always got her way, but there she was, married and chained to two kids she never wanted. In court she claimed that she didn't remember doing it, but the neighbor witnessed what happened. He saw Camilla walk out onto the balcony, carrying your baby brother. He saw her deliberately throw the baby over the railing. Not just drop him, but *throw* him two stories to the ground. He was only three weeks old, Julia, a beautiful boy with blue eyes, just like yours. I thank God that I was babysitting you that day." Val takes a deep breath and looks at me. "Or you might be dead, too."

3

Rain taps my kitchen window and drips its watery fingers down the glass as Lily and I make oatmeal-and-raisin cookies for her preschool party tomorrow. In an era when every child seems to be allergic to eggs or gluten or nuts, making cookies feels like a subversive act, as if I'm crafting poison disks for the delicate darlings. The other mothers are probably preparing healthy snacks like sliced fruit and raw carrots, but I mix butter and eggs, flour and sugar into a greasy dough, which Lily and I drop in clumps onto baking sheets. After the cookies emerge warm and fragrant from the oven, we go into the living room, where I set two cookies, along with a glass of apple juice, in front of Lily for her afternoon snack. Yum, sugar; what a bad mother I am.

She's happily munching away as I sit down at my music stand. I've scarcely taken my instrument out of the case in days, and I need to practice before our quartet's next rehearsal. The violin rests like an old friend on my shoulder and when I tune, the wood sounds mellow and chocolate-rich, a voice that calls for something slow and sweet to warm up with. I set aside the Shostakovich quartet arrangement I planned to practice and instead clip *Incendio* to the stand. Fragments of this waltz have been playing in my head all week, and this morning I woke up hungry to hear it again, to confirm that it's as beautiful as I remember.

And oh yes, it is. The sorrowful voice from my violin seems to sing of broken hearts and lost love, of dark forests and haunted hills. The sorrow turns to agitation. The underlying melody has not changed, but now the notes come faster, move up the scale to the E string, where they scamper up a series of arpeggios. My pulse quickens, along with the frantic pace. I struggle to stay on tempo, my fingers stumbling over one another. My hand cramps. Suddenly the notes fall out of tune and the wood begins to hum as if vibrating at some forbidden frequency that will make my instrument splinter and fly apart. Yet I struggle on, battling my violin, willing it to surrender to me. The hum grows louder, the melody rising to a shriek.

But it's my own scream I hear.

Gasping in agony, I look down at my thigh. At the gleaming shard of glass that protrudes like a crystal dagger from my flesh. Through my own sobs, I hear someone chanting two words over and over in a voice so flat, so mechanical, that I scarcely recognize it. Only when I see her lips moving do I realize it is my own daughter speaking. She stares at me with eyes that are a placid, unearthly blue.

I take three deep breaths for courage and grasp the shard of glass. With a cry, I wrench it out of my thigh. Fresh blood streams down my leg in a bright, scarlet ribbon. It's the last thing I register before everything fades to black.

Through the haze of painkillers, I can hear my husband talking to Val on the other side of the ER privacy curtain. He sounds like he's out of breath, as if he's run into the hospital. Val is trying to calm him down.

"She's going to be fine, Rob. She needed stitches and a tetanus booster shot. And there's a big goose egg on her forehead from hitting the coffee table when she fainted. But after she woke up, she was able to call me for help. I drove right over and brought her straight here."

"Then it's nothing more serious? You're sure she just fainted?"

"If you saw that blood on the floor, you'd understand why she keeled over. It was a pretty scary wound, and it must've hurt like hell. But the ER doctor said it looks clean, and infection shouldn't be an issue."

"Then I can take her home?"

"Yes, yes. Except . . ."

"What?"

Val's voice drops to a murmur. "I'm worried about her. In the car, she told me—"

"Mommy?" I hear Lily whimper. "I want Mommy!"

"Shhh, Mommy's resting, darling. We have to be quiet. No, Lily, stay here. Lily, don't!"

The privacy curtain jerks open and suddenly there is my angelic daughter, reaching up for me. I flinch away, shuddering at her touch. "Val!" I call out. "*Please* take her."

My aunt scoops Lily into her arms. "I'll keep her with me tonight, okay? Hey, Lil', we're going to have a sleepover at my house. Won't that be fun?"

Lily's still reaching for me, begging for a hug, but I turn away, afraid to look at her, afraid to glimpse that blue, alien stare. As Val takes my daughter out of the room I remain frozen on my side. My body feels encased in ice so thick that I don't think I'll ever break free of it. Rob stands beside me, uselessly stroking my hair, but I can't even feel his touch.

"Why don't I take you home now, babe?" he says. "We can order in a pizza and have a quiet evening, just the two of us."

"Juniper wasn't an accident," I whisper.

"What?"

"She attacked me, Rob. She did it on purpose."

His hand pauses on my head. "Maybe it seemed that way to you, but she's only three years old. She's too young to understand what she did."

"She took a piece of broken glass. She *stabbed* me."

"How did she get hold of glass?"

"This morning, I dropped a vase and broke it. I threw the pieces in the trash can. She must have gone into the bag and found them."

"And you didn't see her do it?"

"Why does it sound like you're blaming me?"

"I'm—I'm just trying to understand how this could have happened."

"I'm *telling* you what happened. She did it on purpose. She told me so."

"What did she say?"

"Two words, over and over, like a chant. *Hurt Mommy.*"

He looks at me as if I'm a madwoman, as if I might leap up from the bed and attack him, because no sane woman is afraid of her own three-year-old child. He shakes his head, not knowing how to explain the scene I've just described. Even Rob cannot solve this particular equation.

"Why would she do that?" he finally says. "Just now, she was crying out for you, trying to hug you. She *loves* you."

"I don't know anymore."

"Whenever she's hurt, whenever she's sick, who does she call for? It's always you. You're the center of her universe."

"She heard me screaming. She saw my blood, and she was utterly calm about it. I looked into her eyes, and I didn't see love there."

He can't hide his disbelief; it's there on his face, as obvious as neon. I might as well have told him that Lily sprouted fangs. "Why don't you rest here for a while, sweetheart? I'm going to go talk to your nurse and see when I can take you home."

He walks out of the room and I close my eyes, exhausted. The pain pills they gave me have fogged my brain, and all I want to do is drop into a deep sleep, but in this busy ER too many phones are ringing, too many voices chatter. I hear gurney wheels squeak by in the hallway, and in some distant room a baby is screaming. A very young baby, by the sound of it. I remember the night I brought Lily into this same ER, when she was only two months old and she had a fever. I remember her hot, flushed cheeks and how quiet she was, so very quiet, lying on the exam table. That's what frightened me most, that she didn't cry. Suddenly I ache for that baby, for the Lily I remember. I close my eyes and can smell her hair, feel my lips against the downy top of her head.

"Mrs. Ansdell?" a voice calls.

I open my eyes and see a pale young man standing beside my gurney. He has wire-rim glasses and a white lab coat and his name tag says "Dr. Eisenberg," but he doesn't look old enough to be a medical professional. He doesn't look old enough to be out of high school.

"I just spoke with your husband. He thought I should have a chat with you, about what happened today."

"I've already told the other doctor. I've forgotten his name."

"That was the ER doctor. He was focused on attending to your wound. I want to talk to you about how this injury happened, and why you think your daughter did it."

"Are you a pediatrician?"

"I'm a resident in psychiatry."

"Specializing in children?"

"No, adults. I understand you're very upset."

"I see." I give a weary laugh. "My daughter stabs

me, so of course *I'm* the one who needs the psychiatrist."

"Is that how it happened? She stabbed you?"

I tug aside the bedsheet to reveal my thigh, where the freshly sutured wound is now dressed with gauze. "I know I didn't imagine these stitches."

"I read the ER doctor's note, and it sounds like you got a pretty nasty laceration there. What about that bruise I see on your forehead?"

"I fainted. The sight of blood always makes me dizzy. I think I hit my head on the coffee table."

He pulls up a stool and settles onto it. With his long legs and skinny neck he looks like a stork perched beside my gurney. "Tell me about your daughter, Lily. Your husband said she's three years old."

"Yes. Just."

"Has she ever done anything like this before?"

"There was another incident. About two weeks ago."

"The cat. Yes, your husband told me."

"So you know we have a problem. You know this isn't the first time."

He tilts his head, as though I'm some odd new creature he's trying to figure out. "Are you the only one who's witnessed this behavior of hers?"

His question puts me on guard. Does he think it's all a matter of interpretation? That someone else would have seen something entirely different? It's only natural that he assumes a three-year-old is innocent. A few weeks ago, I would never have believed that my own daughter, with whom I have traded so many hugs and kisses, was capable of violence.

"You haven't met Lily, have you?" I ask.

"No, but your husband tells me she's a very happy, charming little girl."

"She is. Everyone who meets her thinks she's adorable."

"And when you look at her, what do you see?"

"She's my daughter. Of course I think she's perfect in every way. But . . ."

"But?"

My throat chokes to a whisper. "She's different. She's changed."

He says nothing but starts to scribble notes on his clipboard. Pen and paper, how old-fashioned; every other doctor I meet these days types away on a laptop. His handwriting looks like ants marching across the page. "Tell me about the day your daughter was born. Were there any complications? Any difficulties?"

"It was a long labor. Eighteen hours. But everything went fine."

"And how did you feel about giving birth?"

"You mean, aside from being exhausted?"

"I mean emotionally. When you first saw her. When you first held her in your arms."

"You're asking whether we bonded, aren't you? If I wanted her."

He watches, waiting for me to answer my own question. Just my *interpretation* of what he's asking is a sort of Rorschach test, and I sense minefields everywhere. What if I say the wrong thing? Do I become the Bad Mommy?

"Mrs. Ansdell," he says gently, "there is no wrong answer."

"Yes, I wanted my daughter!" I blurt out. "Rob and I tried for years to have a baby. When Lily was born, it was the best day of my life."

"So you were happy about it."

"Of course I was happy! And . . ." I pause. "A little scared."

"Why?"

"Because suddenly, I was responsible for this little person, someone with her own soul. Someone I didn't really know yet."

"When you looked at her, what did you see?"

"A beautiful little girl. Ten fingers, ten toes. Hardly any hair," I add with a wistful laugh, "but perfect in every way."

"You said she was someone with her own soul. Someone you didn't know yet."

"Because newborns are so unformed and you have no idea how they'll turn out. Whether they'll love you. All you can do is wait and see who they grow up to be."

He's scratching on his clipboard again. Obviously I've said something he finds interesting. Was it the bit about babies and souls? I'm not the least bit religious and I have no idea why that spilled out of my mouth. I watch with growing uneasiness, wondering when this ordeal will be over. The local anesthetic has worn off and my wound aches. While this psychiatrist takes his time writing God knows what about me, I'm more and more desperate to escape the glare of these lights.

"What sort of soul do you think Lily has?" he asks.

"I don't know."

He looks up, eyebrow raised, and I realize that my answer was not what he expected. A normal, loving mother would insist her daughter is gentle or kind or innocent. My answer leaves open other, darker possibilities.

"What was she like as a baby?" he asks. "Did she have colic? Any trouble feeding or sleeping?"

"No, she hardly ever cried. She was always happy, always smiling. Always wanting hugs. I never thought motherhood would be so easy, but it was."

"And as she got older?"

"She never went through the terrible twos. She was the perfect child until . . ." I look down at the bedsheet that covers my wounded leg, and my voice fades.

"Why do you think she attacked you, Mrs. Ansdell?"

"I don't know. We were having such a wonderful day. We'd just baked cookies together. She was sitting at the coffee table, drinking her juice."

"And you think she got the piece of glass out of the trash can?"

"That's where she must have gotten it."

"You didn't see it?"

"I was practicing my violin. My eyes were on the music."

"Oh yes. Your husband told me you're a professional musician. Do you play with an orchestra?"

"I'm second violin in a quartet. It's an all-women

group." He merely nods, and I feel compelled to add: "We performed in Rome a few weeks ago."

That seems to impress him. An international gig always impresses people, until they find out how little we're paid to perform.

"When I practice, I'm very focused," I explain. "That's probably why I didn't notice Lily get up and go into the kitchen."

"Do you think she resents the time you spend practicing? Children often hate it when Mom talks on the phone or works on the computer, because they want her full attention."

"It never bothered her before."

"Maybe something was different this time? Maybe you were more focused than usual."

I think about it for a moment. "Well, the music *was* frustrating me. It's a new piece and it's challenging. I'm having trouble with the second half." I pause, as the memory comes back to me of how I struggled to play the waltz. How my fingers cramped as those malevolent notes spun out of my control. The title *Incendio* means "fire" in Italian, but my fingers feel like icicles.

"Mrs. Ansdell, is something wrong?"

"Two weeks ago—the day Lily killed our cat—I was playing that same piece of music."

"What music is this?"

"It's a waltz I brought home from Italy. A handwritten composition I found in an antiques store. What if that's not a coincidence?"

"I doubt we can blame her behavior on a piece of music."

I'm agitated now, obsessed by this new train of

thought. "I've practiced other violin pieces that were just as demanding, and Lily never misbehaved, never complained when I practiced. But there's something different about this waltz. I've played it only twice, and both times, she did something awful."

For a moment he doesn't speak, doesn't write on his clipboard. He just looks at me, but I can almost see the gears furiously spinning in his head. "Describe this music. You said it's a waltz?"

"It's quite haunting, in the key of E minor. Do you know anything about music?"

"I play the piano. Go on."

"The tune begins very quietly and simply. I almost wonder if it was originally written as music to be danced to. But then it grows more and more complex. There are strange accidentals and a series of devil's chords."

"What does that mean, *devil's chords*?"

"They're also called tritones or augmented fourths. In medieval times, these chords were considered evil and banned from church music because they're so dissonant and disturbing."

"This waltz doesn't sound all that pleasant to listen to."

"And it's challenging to play, especially when it climbs into the stratosphere."

"So the notes are high-pitched?"

"In a range that's higher than second violinists usually play."

Again he pauses. Something I've said has clearly intrigued him, and a moment goes by before he says: "When you were playing this piece, at what point did Lily attack you? Was it during those high notes?"

"I think it was. I know I had already turned to the second page."

I watch him tap his pen on the clipboard, a nervous metronomic beat. "Who is Lily's pediatrician?" he suddenly asks.

"Dr. Cherry. We saw him just a week ago for her checkup, and he said she's perfectly healthy."

"Nevertheless, I think I'll give him a call. If it's all right with you, I'm going to suggest a neurology consultant."

"For Lily? Why?"

"It's just a hunch, Mrs. Ansdell. But you may have come up with a very important clue. That piece of music could be the key to everything that's happened."

That night Rob is sound asleep when I climb out of bed and make my way downstairs to the living room. He has cleaned up the bloodstains and the only evidence of what happened to me earlier that day is a damp spot on the carpet. The music stand is right where I left it, with its copy of *Incendio*.

In the soft lamplight, the notes are difficult to see, so I carry the page to the kitchen table and sit down to examine it more closely. I don't know what it is I should be looking for. It is just an ordinary piece of manuscript paper covered on both sides with musical notes, written in pencil. On every page I spot clues to the haste with which this piece was composed: slurs represented by mere slashes, notes that are little more than pencil pricks on a stave. I see no black magic here, no hidden runes or watermarks. But something about this music has infected our lives and changed our daughter into someone who attacks me. Someone who's frightened me.

Suddenly I want to destroy this page. I want to burn it, reduce it to ashes so it cannot hurt us.

I carry it to the stove, turn the knob, and watch the burner's blue flames whoosh to life. But I cannot bring myself to do it. I cannot destroy what might be the only copy in the world of a waltz that enchanted me from the first time I saw it.

I turn off the stove.

Standing alone in my kitchen, I stare at the music and I feel its power radiating from the page like heat from a flame.

And I wonder: *Where did you come from?*

Lorenzo ✎

4

Venice, Before the War

On the day that Professor Alberto Mazza discovered a tiny crack in the face of his beloved violin, a family heirloom made in Cremona two centuries earlier, he knew that only the best luthier in Venice should repair it, and so he headed at once to Bruno Todesco's shop on Calle della Chiesa. With sculpture knife and woodworker's plane, Bruno was known to transform spruce and maple into instruments that came alive with the stroke of a bow across strings. From dead wood he conjured voices, and not just ordinary voices; his instruments sang with such beauty that they were played in orchestras from London to Vienna.

When Alberto stepped into the shop, the violinmaker was so engrossed at his worktable that he did not notice that a new customer had entered. Alberto watched Bruno sand the carved surface of spruce, massaging it as if it were a lover, and noted the fierce focus with which the luthier worked, his whole body craned forward, as if trying to breathe his own soul into the wood so it would come alive and sing for him. An idea suddenly bloomed in Alberto's head, something that had not even occurred to him until this very moment. Here, he thought, was a true artist, devoted to his craft. By reputation, Bruno was a man of temperate habits, industrious, and never known to be in debt. His attendance at synagogue was irregular, true, but he did make the occasional appearance and he never failed to nod deferentially to his elders.

As Bruno labored over the delicate shell of spruce, still unaware of his customer, Alberto slowly perused the shop. A row of gleaming violins hung suspended by their scrolls, all of them fitted with bridges and strings and ready to be played. Beneath the spotless glass countertop were neat rows of rosin boxes and spare bridges and string packets. Against the back wall of the workroom were boards of seasoned spruce and maple, waiting to be carved and shaped into instruments. Everywhere he looked, Alberto saw order and discipline. It was the shop of a man who was not prone to sloppiness, who valued his tools, and who could be relied upon to care about the important details in life. Although Bruno was not yet forty, his hair was already thinning at the crown, his height was merely average, and he would never be considered handsome. But he did have one indispensable qualification.

He was not married.

Here was where their interests aligned. Alberto's thirty-five-year-old daughter, Eloisa, was unmarried as well. Neither beautiful nor homely, she had no suitors in sight, and unless something was done about it, she would die a spinster. Industrious Bruno, laboring at his workbench, was oblivious to the marital net about to be tossed over his head. Alberto wanted grandchildren, and for that he needed a son-in-law.

Bruno would do nicely.

At the wedding eight months later, Alberto brought out the venerable Cremona violin that Bruno had repaired for him. He played the joyous tunes of celebration that his own grandfather had taught him decades before, the same tunes that he later played for the three children born to Eloisa and Bruno. First born was Marco, who came into the world squalling and kicking and punching, already angry at life. Three years later there was Lorenzo, who almost never cried because he was too busy listening, his head turning to the sound of every voice, every birdcall, every note that Alberto played. Ten years later, when Eloisa was forty-nine and certain there would be no more babies for her, little Pia the miracle daughter slid into their world. Here were the precious grandchildren that Alberto had longed for, two boys and a girl, all of them far more handsome than he'd expected, considering their utterly average-looking parents.

But of those three children, only Lorenzo showed signs of musical talent.

At two years old, after hearing a melody only twice, the boy could sing it, so deeply etched was it into his memory, like the grooves on a phonograph record. At five, he could play the same tune on his little quarter-size violin, which was crafted specially for him by his father in the shop on Calle della Chiesa. At eight, whenever Lorenzo practiced in his room, passersby on Calle del Forno would stop to listen to the music drifting out the window. Few could have guessed that such perfect notes were produced by a child's hands, on a child's violin. Lorenzo and his grandfather Alberto often played duets, and the melodies pouring from that window drew listeners from as far away as the Ghetto Vecchio. Some people were so moved by those pure, sweet notes that they wept in the street.

When Lorenzo turned sixteen, he could play Paganini's Capriccio #24, and Alberto knew the time had come. Such demanding music deserved to be played on a fitting instrument, and Alberto placed his cherished Cremona violin in the boy's hands.

"But it's your violin, Grandpapa," said Lorenzo.

"Now it belongs to you. Your brother Marco cares nothing about music, only about his politics. Pia would rather dream her life away, hoping for a fairy-tale prince. But you have the gift. You will know how to make her sing." He nodded. "Go on, boy. Let's hear you play it."

Lorenzo lifted the violin to his shoulder. For a moment he simply held it there, as if waiting for the wood to meld itself to his flesh. The instrument had been passed down through six generations, and the same ebony chin rest had once pressed against the jaw of his grandfather's grandfather. Stored in the memory of this wood were all the melodies that had ever been played on it, and now it was time for Lorenzo to add his own.

The boy stroked the bow across the strings and the notes that sprang from that varnished box of spruce and maple sent a thrill through Alberto. The first piece Lorenzo played was an old Gypsy tune that he'd learned when he was only four, and now he played it slowly, to hear how every note made the wood ring. Next he played a sprightly Mozart sonata, then a Beethoven rondo, and finally he ended with Paganini. Through the window, Alberto saw people gathering below, their heads lifted to the glorious sounds.

When Lorenzo finally lowered his bow, the impromptu audience burst into applause.

"Yes," Alberto murmured, stunned by his grandson's performance. "Oh yes, she was meant to be yours."

"She?"

"She has a name, you know: La Dianora, the Sorceress. It's the name my grandfather gave her when he was struggling to master her. He claimed she fought him at every measure, every note. He never did learn to play well, and he blamed it all on her. He said she obeys only those who are destined to own her. When he gave her to me, and heard the notes I could coax from her, he said: 'She was always meant to be yours.' Just as I say to you now." Alberto placed his hand on Lorenzo's shoulder. "She's yours until you pass her on to your son or grandson. Or perhaps a daughter." Alberto smiled. "Keep her safe, Lorenzo. She's meant to last many lifetimes, not just your own."

5

June 1938

"My daughter has a fine ear and excellent technique on the cello, but I'm afraid she lacks focus and perseverance," said Professor Augosto Balboni. "There is nothing like the prospect of public performance to bring out the best in a musician, and perhaps this will be the motivation she needs." He looked at Lorenzo. "This is why I thought of you."

"What do you think, boy?" Alberto asked his grandson. "Would you do my old friend here a small favor, and play a duet with his daughter?"

Lorenzo looked back and forth at Alberto and the professor, desperately trying to come up with an excuse to bow out. When they'd called him down to the parlor, he'd had no idea this was the reason he'd been asked to join them for coffee. Mama had laid out cake and fruit and sugar-dusted biscuits, evidence of her high regard for Professor Balboni, who was Alberto's colleague in the music department at Ca' Foscari. With his finely tailored suits and his lion's mane of blond hair, Balboni was both impressive and more than a little intimidating. While Alberto seemed to shrink with age every year, Balboni was still in his masculine prime, a man with big gestures and big appetites, who laughed loudly and often. During his frequent visits with Alberto, Balboni's booming voice could be heard all the way up to Lorenzo's bedroom on the third floor.

"Your grandfather tells me you might enter the music competition at Ca' Foscari this year," said Balboni.

"Yes, sir." Lorenzo glanced at Alberto, who offered only an indulgent smile. "Last year, I couldn't compete because I hurt my wrist."

"But it's quite healed now?"

"He sounds even better than before," said Alberto. "And he's learned not to run down those blasted stairs."

"What do you think are your chances of winning the prize?"

Lorenzo shook his head. "I don't know, sir. There are some fine musicians competing."

"Your grandfather says no one is better than you."

"He says that because he is my grandfather."

At this Professor Balboni laughed. "Yes, everyone sees genius under his own roof! But I've known Alberto for more than twenty years, and he's never been one to exaggerate." Balboni took a noisy slurp of coffee and set the cup down on the saucer. "You are, what? Eighteen years old?"

"I turn nineteen in October."

"Perfect. My Laura is seventeen."

Lorenzo had never met the man's daughter and he imagined she looked much like her father, big-boned and loud, with fleshy hands and thick fingers that would slam down hard as hammers against the cello fingerboard. He watched Professor Balboni pluck a sweet biscuit from the tray and bite into it, leaving his mustache coated with sugar. Balboni's hands were large enough to reach an octave-plus-three on the piano, which was no doubt why it was his chosen instrument. On the violin, fingers as thick as his would simply collide with one another.

"Here's my proposal for you, Lorenzo," said Balboni, wiping sugar from his mustache. "You would be doing a great favor to me, and I don't think it would be such a terrible burden for you. The competition is still months away, so there's plenty of time to prepare a duet."

"With your daughter."

"You were already planning to compete at Ca' Foscari, so why not join Laura and enter the violin and cello duet category? For the performance piece, I was thinking perhaps Carlos Maria von Weber, Opus 65, or an arrangement of Beethoven's Rondeau No. 2, Opus 51. Or you might prefer one of the sonatas by Campagnoli. At your advanced level, all of these would be possibilities. Of course it means Laura will have to apply herself, but this is precisely the motivation she needs."

"But I've never even heard her play," said Lorenzo. "I don't know how we'll sound together."

"You have months to rehearse. I'm sure you'll both be ready."

Lorenzo imagined hour after excruciating hour trapped in a stifling room with a clumsy cow of a girl. The agony of listening to her fumble through the notes. The indignity of sharing the stage with her as she mangled Beethoven or von Weber. Oh, he understood what this was all about. Professor Balboni wanted his daughter to be seen at the best possible advantage, and for that she needed a partner skillful enough to disguise her flaws. Surely his grandfather understood what was happening here, and would spare him this ordeal.

But Alberto returned Lorenzo's look with a maddeningly placid smile, as if this arrangement had already been discussed and agreed upon. Professor Balboni was Alberto's best friend; of course Lorenzo must say yes.

"Come to my house on Wednesday, around four o'clock," said Balboni. "Laura will be expecting you."

"But I don't have any of the sheet music you suggested. I'll need time to find copies."

"I have them in my personal library. I'll give them to your grandfather tomorrow, at the college, so you can practice before you come. I have other music at my house, if these pieces don't appeal to you. I'm sure you and Laura can agree on something you both like."

"And if we can't? If we find we're not well matched as musical partners?"

His grandfather gave him a smile of reassurance. "This isn't set in stone. Why don't you meet the girl first?" he suggested. "Then you can decide if you want to go ahead with this."

Shortly before four o'clock on the following Wednesday, Lorenzo carried his violin across the bridge into Dorsoduro. It was a neighborhood favored by professors and academics, and the buildings here were far grander than his own modest home in Cannaregio. He came to the Balbonis' address on Fondamenta Bragadin and halted, intimidated by the massive door with the brass lion's head knocker. Behind him, water slapped in the canal and boats growled past. On the San Vio footbridge, two men stood arguing about which one of them should pay for a damaged wall. Through their agitated voices, he heard a cello playing. The notes seemed to echo from everywhere at once, bounced from brick and stone and water. Did the music come from within the amber-hued walls of Professor Balboni's residence?

He swung the brass knocker and heard the impact reverberate like thunder throughout the house. The door swung open and a woman wearing a scowl and a housekeeper's uniform looked him up and down.

"Excuse me, but I was told to come at four o'clock."

"You're Alberto's grandson?"

"Yes, ma'am. I'm here to rehearse with Miss Balboni."

The woman eyed his violin case and gave a curt nod. "Come with me."

He followed her down a dim hallway, past portraits of men and women whose fleshy features told him they must be Balbonis. In this grand home he felt like an intruder, his leather shoes squeaking across the polished marble.

Timidly he asked the housekeeper: "Is the professor at home?"

"He should be here shortly." The cello music grew louder and the air itself seemed to hum with sonorous notes. "He asked that you two begin the rehearsal without him."

"Miss Balboni and I haven't been introduced yet."

"She's expecting you. There's no need for introductions." The housekeeper swung open double doors and cello music poured out like sweet honey.

Laura Balboni sat near a window, her back turned to him. Against the glare of sunlight all he could see was her silhouette, head bent, shoulders folded forward to embrace her instrument. She played unaware that he stood listening, critically assessing every note that she coaxed from her cello. Her technique was not perfect. Here and there he heard an off-pitch note, and her run of sixteenths was uneven. But her attack was fierce, her bow digging into the strings with such confidence that even her mistakes sounded intentional, every note played without apology. At that moment he did not care what she looked like. She could have the face of a donkey or the hips of a cow. All that mattered was the music that flew from her strings, conjured forth with such passion that the cello seemed at risk of bursting into flame.

"Miss Balboni? The young man is here," announced the housekeeper.

The bow suddenly fell silent. For a moment the girl remained bowed over her instrument, as if reluctant to end the embrace. Then she straightened in her chair and turned to look at him.

"Well," she said after a pause. "You're not the ogre I expected."

"Is that how your father described me?"

"Papa didn't describe you at all. Which is why I expected the worst." She nodded to the housekeeper. "Thank you, Alda. You can shut the door, so we won't disturb you."

The housekeeper withdrew, and Lorenzo was left alone with this strange creature. He had expected a female version of red-faced, bull-necked Professor Balboni, but what he saw was a girl of extraordinary beauty. Her long hair, bright as gold, glittered in the afternoon sunlight. She looked straight at him, but he could not decide if her eyes were blue or green, and he was so distracted by her gaze, he did not immediately notice her arms, where old scars boiled up in ropy masses. Then he saw the marred flesh and although he quickly lifted his gaze back to her face, he couldn't disguise his shock. Any other girl with skin so disfigured would have blushed or looked away or crossed her arms to hide the scars. But Laura Balboni did none of these things. She kept them in full view, as if she were proud of them.

"You play very well," he said.

"You sound surprised."

"To be honest, I didn't know what to expect."

"What did my father tell you about me?"

"Not very much. I must admit, it made me suspicious."

"You were expecting an ogre, too?"

He laughed. "Yes. To be honest."

"And what do you think now?"

What *did* he think? Certainly she was beautiful and talented, but she was also a bit frightening. He'd never met a girl who was so blunt, and her direct gaze left him at a loss for words.

"Never mind. You don't have to answer that." She nodded at his violin case. "Well, aren't you going to take out your instrument?"

"Then you really want to go ahead with this? Prepare a duet?"

"Unless there's something else you'd rather be doing with me."

Flushing, he quickly turned his attention to unpacking the violin. He could feel her studying him and he imagined how unimpressive he must appear, tall and gangly, his shoes scuffed, his collar frayed. He had not dressed with particular care for this visit because he had no interest in impressing Laura-the-ogre. But now that he'd met her, he bitterly regretted not wearing his good shirt, not polishing his shoes. One's first impression is what lasts, and he could never go back and change this day. With a sense of resignation, he tuned his violin and quickly played a few arpeggios to warm up his fingers.

"Why did you agree to this?" she asked.

He focused on rubbing rosin on his bow. "Because your father thought we would make an excellent duo."

"And you said yes, just because he asked you?"

"He's my grandfather's friend and colleague."

"So it was impossible for you to say no." She sighed. "You must be honest with me, Lorenzo. If you truly don't want to do this, just tell me now. I'll tell Papa that I was the one who made the decision. Not you."

He turned to face her, and this time he could not look away. Nor did he want to. "I came here to play music with you," he said. "That's what I think we should do."

She gave a crisp nod. "Then shall we start with von Weber? Just to hear how well our instruments blend together?"

She placed the von Weber score on her music stand. He had neglected to bring his own stand, so he stood behind her and read the page over her shoulder. They were so close, he could smell her scent, sweet as rose petals. Her blouse had puff sleeves edged in lace, and around her neck was a delicate chain from which a tiny cross dangled, just above the top button of her blouse. He knew the Balbonis were Catholic, but the sight of that gold cross gleaming at her breastbone gave him pause.

Before he could slip his violin under his chin, she started in on the first four measures. The tempo was moderato, and her introductory notes sang out, mellow and contemplative. Her arms might be encased in ugly scars, but they could coax magic from the cello. He wondered how she had been burned. A childhood fall into the fireplace? A boiling pot tumbling from the stove? While other girls would wear long sleeves, Laura boldly displayed her disfigurement.

At measure five, his violin came in with the melody. Joined in perfect harmony, they blended into a voice far grander than the mere sum of their instruments. *This* was the way von Weber was meant to sound! But it was a short piece, and too quickly they came to the final measure. Even after they both lifted their bows, their last notes seemed to linger in the air like a plaintive sigh.

Laura looked up at him, her lips parted in astonishment. "I never knew this piece was so beautiful."

He stared at the music on her stand. "I didn't, either."

"Please, let's play it again!"

Behind him came the sound of a throat being cleared. Lorenzo turned to see the housekeeper, Alda, standing with a tray of teacups and biscuits. She did not even glance at him, but looked only at Laura.

"You requested tea, Miss Balboni."

"Thank you, Alda," said Laura.

"Professor Balboni should have arrived home by now."

"You know how he is. Papa's no slave to any schedule. Oh, Alda? I expect there'll be three of us dining tonight."

"Three?" Only then did the housekeeper deign to glance at Lorenzo. "The young man is staying?"

"I'm sorry, Lorenzo. I should have asked you first," Laura said. "Or did you have other plans for dinner tonight?"

He looked back and forth at the girl and her housekeeper, and felt the tension in the room congeal into something thick and ugly. He thought of his mother, who would now be preparing the evening meal. And he thought of the gold cross that dangled from Laura's neck.

"My family is expecting me for dinner. I am afraid I must decline," he said.

Alda's lip curled into a satisfied smile. "So there will be only two tonight, as usual," she said and withdrew from the room.

"Do you have to hurry home so soon? Do you have time to play a few more pieces with me?" Laura said. "My father suggested Campagnoli or the Beethoven rondeau for the competition. Although I confess, I'm not particularly fond of either one."

"Then we should choose something else."

"But I haven't practiced any other music."

"Would you like to try a duet that you haven't practiced?"

"Which duet would that be?"

Lorenzo reached into the side pocket of his instrument case and took out two pages of sheet music, which he set on Laura's stand. "Try this. I think you can sight-read it."

"La Dianora," she said, frowning at the title. "An interesting name for a tune." She picked up her bow and launched into the first measure with gusto.

"No, no! You're playing it much too fast. The tempo is supposed to be adagio. If you start off too quickly, there'll be no surprise when it later changes to presto."

"How would I know that?" she snapped. "It doesn't say adagio anywhere on this page. And I've never seen this music before!"

"Of course you haven't. I've just finished writing it."

She blinked at him in surprise. "This is *your* composition?"

"Yes."

"And why is it called 'La Dianora'? The Sorceress?"

"It's the name of my violin, La Dianora. I'm still revising the second half, because it doesn't sound quite right, but I believe the overall motif is compelling. Also, this arrangement allows both our instruments to shine, and that will be to our advantage in a duet competition."

"Oh, that awful competition!" Laura sighed. "Why must everything be about who's the best, who's number one? I wish we could play music just for the joy of it."

"Aren't you enjoying this now?"

She was silent for a moment as she regarded the music. "Yes," she said, sounding surprised. "Yes, I am enjoying this. But having that competition hanging over our heads—it changes everything."

"Why?"

"Because now it's not about fun. It's about pride. There's something you should know about me, Lorenzo. I don't like to lose, ever." She looked at him. "If we're going to compete for this prize, I have every intention of winning."

6

Every Wednesday for the next two months, Lorenzo walked across the bridge to Dorsoduro. At four o'clock, he'd knock at the door on Fondamenta Bragadin and would be ushered in by the eternally sour-faced housekeeper. He and Laura would rehearse "La Dianora," then break for tea and cakes, at which time Professor Balboni sometimes joined them. Afterward they would play whatever music amused them, but at the end of the session, they always returned to "La Dianora," which they had settled upon as their competition piece.

The cello part frustrated Laura. He could see it in her face: her deeply etched frown, her squared jaw. "Again!" she'd demand after she'd stumbled through a difficult passage. And after the next flawed run-through: "Again!" And: "Again!" This girl was so fierce that she sometimes scared him. Then she'd burst out in delighted laughter when, after an hour of struggling over that cursed passage, she'd suddenly get it right. In the span of a

single afternoon, she could surprise and frustrate
and enchant him.

No longer was Wednesday a day like any other.
Now he thought of them as *Laura* days, when he'd
step into her house, her world, and forget about his
own. When he could sit knee to knee with her, close
enough to see the glow of perspiration on her face
and hear her soft intake of breath as she attacked
the strings with her bow. A duet was far more than
two instruments playing notes together. It was also
about joining in perfect harmony, about linking
minds and hearts so completely that you know the
precise instant when your partner will lift her bow
and let the final note die.

As the competition drew near, they were close to
achieving that perfection. Lorenzo pictured the
two of them onstage at Ca' Foscari, their instruments gleaming under the lights, Laura's gown
pooling on the floor around her chair. He imagined
their flawless performance and the triumphant
smile on her face. He and Laura would join hands
onstage and take bow after bow as the audience
applauded.

Then they'd pack up their instruments, say goodbye to each other, and that would be the end of it.
No more rehearsals, no more afternoons with
Laura. *I must remember this moment. After we go
our separate ways, these memories are all I'll have
left of her.*

"Oh for heaven's sakes, Lorenzo!" she snapped.
"Where is your head today?"

"Sorry. I lost track of which measure we're on."

"Measure twenty-six. You did something odd

there, and now we're not together." She frowned at him. "Is something wrong?"

"Nothing." He rotated his shoulder, massaged his neck. "It's just that we've been at this for hours now."

"Shall we stop for tea again?"

"No, let's just push on."

"Are you in a hurry to leave?"

Leaving her was the last thing he wanted to do, but it was nearly eight o'clock and the scent of dinner had begun wafting in from the kitchen. "It's late. I don't want to overstay my welcome."

"I understand." She sighed. "Oh well. I know you find it hard to be trapped here with me."

"Excuse me?"

"We don't *have* to like each other. We just have to play well together, right?"

"What makes you think I don't like being with you?"

"Isn't it obvious? Three times I've invited you to stay for dinner. Every time, you've declined."

"Laura, you don't understand—"

"What should I understand?"

"I assumed you were just trying to be polite when you invited me."

"Polite would be *one* invitation. *Three* invitations surely goes beyond mere politeness."

"I'm sorry. I know that Alda isn't comfortable having me here, and I didn't want to make things difficult."

"Did Alda actually *say* this to you?"

"No. But I can see it in her face. The way she looks at me."

"Ah, so now you're a mind reader. You take one look at Alda and you know *exactly* what she's thinking. And oh dear, she *disapproves* of you, so of course you don't dare accept my invitations. Are you so easily discouraged by everything in life, Lorenzo?"

He stared back at her, stung by the truth of what she'd said. Laura would never be so easily intimidated. She was braver than he could ever be, brave enough to wave her ugly scars like scarlet flags. Now she was challenging him to be as bold as she was, and to say exactly what he thought, whatever the consequences.

Grimly she set down her cello. "You're right," she said. "It's getting late. I'll see you next week."

"I *do* like being with you, Laura. In fact, there's no place I'd rather be than right here."

"Is this the real Lorenzo talking? Or is this the diplomat Lorenzo, trying to say the polite thing and not offend me?"

"This is the truth," he said quietly. "All week, I look forward to Wednesday and being here with you. But I'm not good at speaking my mind the way you are. You're the bravest girl I've ever met." He looked down at his feet. "I know I'm too cautious, and I always have been. Afraid to do or say the wrong thing. The only time I feel brave, truly brave, is when I'm playing music."

"All right then. We should play." She picked up her cello and bow. "And maybe tonight you'll feel brave enough to stay for dinner."

* * *

"More wine, let's have more wine!" said Professor Balboni, and he refilled their goblets. Was it their fourth glass or their fifth? Lorenzo had lost count, but what did it matter? The evening was one long, happy blur. The music of Duke Ellington played on the phonograph as they dined on Alda's delicate broth with minced vegetables, followed by *fegato* and potatoes, and finally cake and fruits and nuts. Never had Lorenzo enjoyed a meal so much, made all the more delightful because of the people he shared it with. Laura sat across from him, her bare arms in full view, and the sight of her scars no longer startled him. No, those scars were yet another reason he admired her. They were a testament to her courage, to her willingness to reveal exactly who she was, without apology.

Her father was just as forthright with his brash statements and boisterous laughter. Professor Balboni wanted to know their guest's opinions about everything. What did he think of jazz? Did he prefer Louis Armstrong or Duke Ellington? Did he think there was any role for the violin in this modern music?

And then: "What are your plans for the future?"

The future? Lorenzo could scarcely think beyond the competition in three weeks. "I plan to attend Ca' Foscari, like my brother Marco," he said.

"Which subject will you study at the college?"

"Marco advised me to study government. He said I'll be able to find a job."

Professor Balboni snorted. "You would feel buried alive, studying something as dull as government. Music is your field. Aren't you already teaching the violin?"

"Yes, sir, I have seven students, all of them eight or nine years old. My father thinks we should combine our businesses. I teach the violin, and he provides my students with their instruments. He wants me to take over his shop someday, but I don't think I would make a good luthier."

"That's because you're not a woodworker, you're a musician. Something your grandfather recognized since you were just a child. Surely you could find a position in some orchestra? Or you should consider going abroad, to America perhaps."

"America?" Lorenzo laughed. "What a fantasy!"

"Why not dream big? It's not impossible."

"It means leaving my family." He looked across the table at Laura. *It means leaving her.*

"I really think you should consider emigrating, Lorenzo. This country is changing, and all too quickly." Professor Balboni's voice was suddenly quiet. "These are not good times. I have spoken to Alberto about other possibilities, places where your family could settle."

"My grandfather will never leave Italy, and my father can't leave his business. He's built a reputation here and he has loyal clients."

"Yes, for now, his business is probably safe. Skilled luthiers don't just sprout up overnight, so he can't be easily replaced. But who knows what the regime will do next? What new decrees the Interior Ministry might issue?"

Lorenzo nodded. "That's what Marco keeps saying. Every day, he finds something in the news to be outraged about."

"Then your brother is paying attention."

"My father says we shouldn't worry. He says these decrees are political games, just for show, and the regime will never turn against us. We have to trust Mussolini."

"Why?"

"Because he knows we're loyal citizens. He's said it again and again: there is no Jewish question here." Lorenzo took a confident sip of wine. "Italy is not Germany."

"This is what your father says?"

"Yes, and my grandfather as well. They believe Mussolini will always support us."

"Well then, perhaps they are right. I hope they are right." Professor Balboni sank back in his chair, as if the effort to keep up a lively conversation had drained him. "You are an optimist, Lorenzo, like your grandfather. It's why Alberto and I are such excellent friends. No doom and gloom from him, only good cheer, even when the times are not good."

But this evening is surely one of the good times, thought Lorenzo. How could it not be, with Laura smiling at him, the wine flowing, and excellent jazz playing on the phonograph? Even the sight of Alda's chilly expression could not dampen the pleasure of sitting at the Balbonis' table.

It was well past one in the morning when he stepped out their door. Walking the empty streets back to his own neighborhood of Cannaregio, he did not worry about the dangers he might encounter on the way, or whether some roving band of thugs might attack him. No, tonight he was immune to misfortune, walking in a protective cloud of happiness. He had been welcomed into the Balboni family, accepted as their friend, praised as an artist. Laura herself had walked him to the door, and he could still picture her framed in that rectangle of light, waving goodbye. He could still hear her call out: "Until Wednesday, Lorenzo!"

He was humming the melody of "La Dianora" as he walked into his house and hung up his coat and hat.

"What makes *you* so damn happy tonight?" said Marco.

Lorenzo turned and saw his brother standing in the kitchen doorway. He wasn't surprised that Marco was still awake; only after dark did he seem to come fully alive, and he'd stay up half the night arguing politics with his friends, or poring over the latest newspapers and pamphlets. Marco's hair stood up in stiff tufts, as if he'd been plowing his fingers through it. He looked thuggish tonight, his face unshaven, his undershirt untucked and stained.

"Mama and Pia were worried about you," Marco said.

"After rehearsal, they invited me to stay for dinner."

"Did they, now?"

"I had a wonderful time. It was the best evening ever!"

"Is that all it takes to make you happy? Being allowed to stay at their house for dinner?"

"Not allowed. *Invited.* There's a difference, you

know." As Lorenzo started toward the stairs, Marco grasped his arm. "Take care, little brother. You may think they're on your side, but how do you really know?"

Lorenzo shook him off. "Not everyone's against us, Marco. Some people *are* on our side."

He carried his violin up the stairs to his attic bedroom and opened the window to let in fresh air. Even Marco couldn't ruin this night for him. He wanted to sing, to shout out to the world what an evening he had had with Laura and her father. Everything seemed so much happier and brighter in the Balboni household, where wine flowed and jazz played and all seemed possible. *Why not dream big?* Professor Balboni had challenged him.

That night, lying in bed, Lorenzo did just that. He dared to dream about America, about Laura, about a future together. Yes, it all seemed possible.

Until the next day, when Professor Balboni knocked on their door with news that changed their lives.

7

"How can Ca' Foscari do this to me?" said Alberto. "For thirty-five years, I've taught there! Now they dismiss me without any reason, without any warning?"

"There were plenty of warnings, Grandpapa," said Marco. "All these months, I've pointed them out to you. You saw the editorials in *Il Tevere*. In *Quadrivio*."

"Those newspapers spew nothing but racist nonsense. No one believed it would lead to any real changes."

"You read the 'Manifesto of the Scientists.' That was certainly a warning of things to come. Now it's all coming to pass."

"But for the college to dismiss me, without cause?"

"They *have* their cause. You're a Jew and that's reason enough for them."

Alberto turned to his colleague Balboni, who sat shaking his head. The whole family had gathered around the dining table, but there was no food, no refreshment in sight; Lorenzo's mother was so distressed by the news, she'd neglected her duties as a proper hostess and had sunk into a chair, shocked into silence.

Lorenzo's father said: "Surely this is just a temporary measure. An empty gesture to curry favor with Berlin." Bruno, ever the Mussolini fan, refused to believe Il Duce would ever turn against them. "And what about Professor Leone? His wife isn't a Jew, and this will punish her as well. Mark my words, in a few weeks, it will be reversed. The college can't function without its Jewish faculty."

Marco flung up his hands in frustration. "Papa, did you not read the memorandum? This order applies to *students* as well. We're now expelled from every school in Italy!"

"They did allow one small mercy," said Professor Balboni. "They made an exception for students in their final year, so you will be allowed to finish your studies, Marco. But Lorenzo?" He shook his head. "He can't enroll at Ca' Foscari, or any other college in Italy."

"Even if I am allowed to finish," said Marco, "what good is my degree? No one will hire me now." His eyes suddenly glimmered with tears and he turned away. How diligently he'd studied, always so certain of his path in life. He would serve Italy like his heroes Volpi and Luzzatti. He'd dreamed of working as a diplomat, and he'd debated which languages he should study, wondered in which countries he'd someday work. At eight years old, he'd tacked a map of the world on his wall, a map that he'd traced so often with his fingers that parts of the paper had been rubbed away. Now those hopes were dead because Italy had betrayed him; Italy had betrayed them all.

Marco gave his eyes an angry swipe. "And look what they've done to poor Grandpapa! Half his life, he taught at Ca' Foscari. Now he is nothing."

"He is still a teacher, Marco," said Balboni.

"A teacher with no income. Oh, but Jews don't need to eat. We can live on air, can't we?"

"Marco," warned his mother. "Be respectful. Professor Balboni isn't responsible for this."

"What are he and his colleagues going to do about it?"

"We are appalled, of course," said Balboni. "We've written a petition of protest. I've signed it, and so have dozens of others on the faculty."

"Dozens? Not everyone?"

Balboni lowered his head. "No," he admitted. "Some are afraid of repercussions if they sign. And others . . ." He shrugged. "Well, they were never your friends, anyway. And now there are rumors that more bad news is coming. New laws being proposed, affecting Jews in other professions. I tell you, it all springs from that damned 'Manifesto of the Scientists.' It unleashed this madness. It gave everyone permission to blame you for all the ills in the country."

Published a month earlier in *Il Giornale d'Italia,* the manifesto had sent Marco into a rage. He'd stormed into the house waving the newspaper, shouting: "Now they say we're not true Italians! They say we're a foreign race!" Since then he had talked of little else. He had brought home pamphlets and newspapers to pore over at night, feeding his anger. Every family meal turned into a battleground because his father and grandfather remained loyal fascists, unwilling to believe that Mussolini would turn against them. The arguments at dinner grew so heated that once, to everyone's shock, Mama had slapped a knife down on the table and declared: "Enough! If you're going to kill each other, why not use that knife! At least it will finally be quieter around here!"

Now another argument was about to explode and Lorenzo saw angry veins bulge on his brother's neck, saw Mama's hands tense into claws on the table.

"There must be a way to appeal this memorandum," said Alberto. "I will write a letter to the newspaper."

"Oh yes," Marco snorted. "A letter will change everything!"

Bruno gave his son a slap on the head. "And what would *you* do? You're so brilliant, Marco, I'm sure *you* have all the answers!"

"At least I'm not blind and deaf, like everyone else in this family!" Marco stood, shoving his chair back so hard it toppled over backward. He left it lying on the floor and stormed out of the room.

His sister, Pia, jumped up to follow him. "Marco!" she called. "Please don't leave. I hate it when you all fight like this!" They heard her run out the door, heard her calling out as she pursued her brother. Of them all, nine-year-old Pia was the true diplomat in the family, always distressed when they argued, always anxious to negotiate peace. Even as her voice faded down the street, she was still beseeching her brother to return.

Inside the house, a long and heavy silence passed.

"So what are we to do now?" Eloisa asked softly.

Professor Balboni shook his head. "There is nothing you can do. My colleagues and I will present our petition to the college. Some of us are composing letters to the newspaper as well, but we have little hope they'll be published. Everyone's nervous, everyone fears a backlash. There could be reprisals against those who disagree with the regime."

"We have to loudly and publicly declare our loyalty," said Alberto. "Remind them of everything we've done for the country. All the wars we've served in, defending Italy."

"It makes no difference, my friend. Your Jewish Union has issued press release after press release, declaring its loyalty. What good has it done?"

"Then what else can we say? What can we do?"

Professor Balboni considered his next words, and his whole body seemed to sag with the weight of his answer. "You should consider leaving the country."

"Leave Italy?" Alberto stiffened in his chair, outraged. "My family has lived here for four hundred years. I'm as Italian as you are!"

"I'm not arguing with you, Alberto. I'm only giving you advice."

"What sort of advice is that? To abandon our country? Do you think so little of our friendship that you'd shove us onto the next boat?"

"Please, you don't understand—"

"Understand *what*?"

Professor Balboni's voice dropped to a murmur. "There are rumors," he said. "Things I've heard from my colleagues abroad."

"Yes, we've all heard the rumors. That's all they are, spread by those crazy Zionists to make us turn against the regime."

"But I'm hearing the stories from people I know to be levelheaded," said Professor Balboni. "They say there are things going on now, in Poland. Reports of mass deportations."

"To where?" asked Eloisa.

"Labor camps." Balboni looked at her. "Women and children, too. All ages, healthy or not, are being arrested and transported. Their homes and possessions have been seized. Some of what I've heard is too horrible to believe, and I won't repeat it. But if it's happening in Poland—"

"It won't happen here," said Alberto.

"You have too much faith in the regime."

"Do you really expect us to leave? Where would we all go?"

"Portugal or Spain. Perhaps Switzerland."

"And how will we feed ourselves in Switzerland?" Alberto pointed to his son-in-law, who was clearly struggling to process this new upheaval in their lives. "Bruno has loyal clients. He's spent his whole life building a reputation."

"We won't leave," Bruno abruptly declared. He sat up straight and looked at his wife. "Your father is right. Why should we leave? We've done nothing wrong."

"But these rumors," said Eloisa. "Think of Pia in a labor camp. . . ."

"Would it be better for her to starve in Switzerland?"

"Oh my God. I don't know what we should do."

But Bruno did. This was his household, and although he seldom asserted himself, now he made it clear that he was in charge. "I won't leave everything I've worked for. My shop is here, my clients are here. And Lorenzo has his violin students. Together, we can make do."

Alberto placed a hand on his son-in-law's shoulder. "Good, we're in agreement, then. We stay."

Balboni sighed. "I know it was a drastic suggestion that you leave the country, but I had to speak my mind. If events should accelerate, if conditions suddenly grow worse, there may not be another chance to leave. This could be the best opportunity you'll have." He rose from the table. "I'm sorry to have brought you this news, my friend. But I wanted to prepare you, before you hear it from anyone else." He looked at Lorenzo. "Come, young man, take a walk with me. Let's discuss how your rehearsals with Laura are going."

Lorenzo followed him outside, but the professor didn't say a word as they walked together toward the canal. He seemed deep in thought, his hands clasped behind him, his brow furrowed.

"I don't want to leave Italy, either," said Lorenzo.

Balboni shot him a distracted look, as if surprised he was still there beside him. "No, of course you don't. No one wants to be uprooted. I wouldn't expect you to say otherwise."

"Yet you advise us to leave."

Professor Balboni halted in the narrow street and faced him. "You are a levelheaded boy, Lorenzo. Unlike your brother Marco, who I fear will do something rash and bring disaster down on all your heads. Your grandfather has always spoken highly of you. I've seen for myself that you have great promise as a musician, and as a man. Which is why I urge you to pay attention to what's happening all around us. Whatever your brother's faults, at least he sees the pattern that's developing. So should you."

"The pattern?"

"Have you not noticed how all the newspapers now speak with one voice, and that voice is raised against Jews? The movement has been building steadily for years. A newspaper editorial here, an official memorandum there. As if this is all a carefully planned campaign."

"Grandfather says it's just ignorant people making noise."

"Beware the ignorant, Lorenzo. They're the most dangerous enemy of all, because they are everywhere."

They did not speak of the matter when Lorenzo came to rehearse the following Wednesday, nor on the Wednesday after that. He dined with the Balbonis both times, but their conversations over dinner were strictly about music: the latest records they had listened to. What did Lorenzo think about Shostakovich? Did everyone plan to see the new musical comedy with Vittorio De Sica? And how sad to hear that the distinguished luthier Oreste Candi had passed away in Genoa. It was as if they were trying their best to avoid talking about the storm clouds gathering over their heads, so instead they chattered about the pleasant and the trivial.

Yet the subject still lurked in the room, as ominous as the grim face of Alda, who silently slipped in and out, clearing the table between courses. Lorenzo wondered why the Balbonis chose to keep such an unfriendly woman in their employ. He'd gathered that Alda had been with the family since before Laura was born, and had been the personal maid to Laura's mother, who had died of blood cancer ten years ago. Perhaps after all those years, the Balbonis had simply grown accustomed to that stone face, the way you learn to live with a club-foot or a bad knee.

Three days before the competition, Lorenzo dined with the Balbonis one last time.

Their final run-through had gone exceedingly well, so well that the professor shot to his feet and applauded. "No other duo comes close!" he declared. "Your instruments are like two souls joined together, singing as one. Tonight, why don't we celebrate your victory? I'll open a special bottle of wine."

"We haven't won the prize yet, Papa," Laura said.

"Merely a formality. They should already be writing your names on the certificate." He poured the wine and handed goblets to his daughter and Lorenzo. "If you both play as well as you did tonight, you cannot lose." He winked. "I know that, because I've heard the other contestants."

"How, Papa? When?" asked Laura.

"Today, at the college. Professor Vettori has been coaching some of the other duos. While they played, I just *happened* to be standing outside the rehearsal room."

"Naughty Papa!"

"What, was I supposed to cover my ears and block them out? They were playing so loudly I could hear every sour note." He held up his goblet. "Come, let's have a toast."

"To the prize," said Laura.

"To competent judges!" said her father.

Laura beamed at Lorenzo. Never had he seen her so beautiful, her face flushed from the wine, her hair like liquid gold in the lamplight. "And what do *you* toast to?" she asked.

To you, Laura, he thought. *To every sacred moment we've shared.*

He raised his glass. "To what brought us together. To music."

Lorenzo paused outside the Balbonis' front door and breathed in the damp night air. Lingering in the cold, he listened to the slap of water in the canal and tried to commit to memory this night, this moment. It was his last visit to their house, and he was not yet ready for it to end. What else did he have to look forward to? Now that he could not enroll at Ca' Foscari, all he saw was an eternity in his father's workshop, sanding and carving wood, building instruments for other musicians. He would grow old in that dim and dusty space, would shrink into a bitter version of his father, Bruno, but Laura's life would go on. For her there would be college and all the pleasures of being a student. There would be parties and concerts and films.

And there would be young men, always circling nearby, hoping to catch her eye. They had only to glimpse her smile, hear the music of her laughter, and they'd be enchanted. She would marry one of those young men, and they'd have children, and she'd forget about the Wednesday afternoons years before, when his violin and her cello had sung together so sweetly.

"This will come to no good. Surely you know that."

Startled by the voice, he spun around so sharply that his violin case scraped the wall. Alda lurked in the shadow of the alley beside the Balbonis' residence, her face barely visible in the glow from a streetlamp.

"End it now," said Alda. "Tell her you can't take part in the competition."

"You want me to quit? What possible reason would I give her?"

"Anything. Use your head."

"We've rehearsed for months. We're ready to perform. Why should I withdraw now?"

Her answer, spoken so softly, held the quiet note of menace. "There'll be consequences if you don't."

Suddenly he laughed. He'd had enough of this gargoyle of a woman, always scowling in the background, always casting her shadow over every happy evening he'd spent with Laura. "That's supposed to frighten me?"

"If you have any sense—if you care about her—it should."

"Why do you think I'm doing this? It's for *her*."

"Then walk away now, before you pull her into dangerous waters. She's an innocent. She has no idea what's about to happen."

"And you do?"

"I know people. They tell me things."

He stared at her with sudden comprehension. "You're one of those Blackshirts, aren't you? Did they tell you to scare the Jew away? Make me scurry off and hide in the gutter like a rat?"

"You don't understand a thing, young man."

"Oh, I do. I understand all too well. But it won't stop me."

As he walked away, he could feel her gaze burning into his back, hot as a poker. Rage propelled him at a furious pace out of Dorsoduro. Alda's warning to stay away from Laura had precisely the opposite effect: He would never withdraw from the competition. No, he was committed to it, and to Laura. This was what Marco had raged on about all these months, that Jews should not yield an inch, that they should demand, even seize, their rights as loyal Italians. Why had he not been paying attention?

Lying in bed, too agitated to sleep, he thought only of winning. What better way to fight back than to triumph at the competition? To demonstrate that by denying him enrollment at Ca' Foscari, the college was depriving itself of the best that

Italy had to offer? Yes, that was how to fight, not with impotent letters to the newspapers as Alberto had suggested, not with the marches and protests that Marco threatened. No, the best way was to work harder and soar higher than anyone else. Prove your worth, and respect will follow.

He and Laura would have to shine so brightly onstage that no one would question they deserved the prize. *That's how we fight. That's how we win.*

8

Laura's satin gown was so black that at first, all he could make out in the shadowy street was a faint shimmering. Then she emerged from the night and suddenly there she stood, lustrous in the glow of the streetlamp. Her blond hair was swept to one side in a waterfall of gold and a short velvet cape draped her shoulders. Her father, who carried her cello case, looked equally elegant in a black suit and bow tie, but Lorenzo could only stare at Laura, resplendent in satin.

"Have you been waiting out here for us?" she asked.

"There's a huge crowd in the auditorium and almost every chair's taken. My grandfather wanted you to know that he's saving a seat for you, Professor. In the fourth row, on the left."

"Thank you, Lorenzo." Professor Balboni looked him up and down and gave a nod of approval. "You'll make a handsome pair onstage, you two. Now hurry inside. This cold air isn't good for your instruments." He handed his daughter the cello. "Remember, don't rush the first measures. Don't let your nerves set the rhythm."

"Yes, Papa, we'll remember," said Laura. "Now you'd better go find your seat."

Balboni gave his daughter a kiss. "Good luck, both of you!" he said and headed into the auditorium.

For a moment, Laura and Lorenzo stood in silence under the streetlamp, staring at each other. "You're beautiful tonight," he said.

"Only tonight?"

"I meant—"

Laughing, she touched two fingers to his lips. "Hush, I know what you meant. You're beautiful tonight, too."

"Laura, even if we don't win, even if everything goes wrong onstage, it doesn't matter. These weeks we've had together—the music we've played—*that's* what I'll always remember."

"Why do you talk as if tonight is the end of something? It's just the beginning. And we start by winning."

Just the beginning. As they entered the stage door, he allowed himself to imagine a future with Laura. Other evenings when they'd walk into concert halls with their instruments in hand. Laura and Lorenzo performing in Rome! Paris! London! He pictured her in the years to come, her hair fading to silver, her face ripening with age, but always, always beautiful. What more perfect future could there be than to live this moment again and again, walking to stage doors with Laura?

The whine of instruments being tuned led them to the greenroom, where the other contestants had assembled. Suddenly the tuning stopped and there was silence as everyone turned to look at them.

Laura removed her velvet cape and opened her cello case. Ignoring the stares, the ominous silence, she gave her bow a few brisk scrapes of rosin and settled into a chair to tune. She didn't even glance up when a formally dressed man quickly crossed the room toward her.

"Miss Balboni, may I have a word with you?" the man murmured.

"Perhaps later, Mr. Alfieri," she said. "Right now, my violinist and I need to warm up."

"I'm afraid there is a . . . complication."

"Is there?"

The man pointedly avoided looking at Lorenzo. "Perhaps, if we could speak in private?"

"You may speak to me right here."

"I have no wish to turn this into an unpleasant scene. Surely you're aware of the recent change in policy. This competition is open only to musicians of the Italian race." He shot a furtive glance at Lorenzo. "Your entry has been disqualified."

"But we're on the printed program." She pulled the sheet of paper from her cello case. "This was announced a month ago. Our names are right here. We're scheduled to perform second."

"The schedule has changed. That is the end of the matter." He turned and walked away.

"No it isn't," she called out, loudly enough so that everyone in the room could hear her. They were all watching as she set down her cello and followed the man across the room. "You haven't given me one good reason why we can't compete."

"I gave you the reason."

"A ridiculous one."

"It was the decision of the committee."

"What, your committee of *sheep*?" Laura gave a brassy laugh. "We are scheduled to perform a duet, Mr. Alfieri. We have every right to perform. Now, if you'll excuse us, my violinist and I need to warm up." She spun away and crossed back to Lorenzo. It was not a walk but a march, her gaze straight ahead, shoulders squared. Her eyes were bright as diamonds, her cheeks flushed as though with fever. The other musicians quickly stepped out of her way to avoid colliding with such a powerful force.

"Let's tune," she commanded.

"Laura, there could be trouble for you," said Lorenzo.

"Do you want to play or not?" she snapped, a challenge flung at him by a girl who did not understand what fear was. Had she thought about the consequences, or was she so bent on winning that the risks didn't matter to her? Dangerous or not, he would stand beside her. They must be fearless together.

He unlatched his case and took out La Dianora. As he raised the violin to his jaw and felt its wood against his skin, his nerves steadied. La Dianora had never failed him; play her well, and she would sing. In the echoing greenroom, her voice soared so warm and rich that the other musicians turned to watch.

Mr. Alfieri called out: "Pirelli and Gayda! You're first. Up to the stage now."

Everyone fell silent as the first pair of contestants picked up their instruments and headed up the stairs.

Cradling La Dianora in his arms, Lorenzo felt the warmth of her wood, as alive as human flesh. He looked at Laura, but she was completely focused on the sound of welcoming applause overhead. Then came the faint strains of the cello, its voice resonating through the wooden stage. She listened intently to the music, her gaze tilted upward, her lip twitching into a smile at the sound of a distinctly sour note. She was as hungry to win as he was. Judging by the shaky performance of this first duo, how could he and Laura *not* win? He tapped the fingerboard, impatient to be onstage.

They heard applause again, as the first pair ended their performance.

"We're next. Let's go," said Laura.

"Stop!" called Mr. Alfieri as they headed up the stairs. "You can't go up there! You're not on the program!"

"Ignore him," said Laura.

"Miss Balboni, I insist you halt at once!"

The first duo had just walked into the wings. Laura and Lorenzo swept right past them and emerged into the glare of stage lights. Lorenzo was so blinded, he could not see the audience. He could only hear their scattered applause, which rapidly died away, leaving him and Laura standing beneath the spotlights in silence. No official came out to introduce them. No one announced their names.

Laura crossed to the cellist's chair, her high heels clacking smartly across the wooden stage. The chair legs gave a noisy scrape as she sat down. Briskly she arranged the hem of her gown and sank the cello end pin into the anchor. Bow poised, she turned to Lorenzo and smiled.

He forgot that hundreds of people were watching them. At that moment, he saw only Laura, and she saw only him.

Their gazes stayed fixed on each other as he raised his bow. So attuned were they to each other, they didn't need to say a word, didn't need to nod an introductory count. They knew, with a musician's instinct, the precise instant when their bows would simultaneously attack the strings. This was their world and theirs alone, the stage lights their sun, their language spoken in the key of G, their notes so perfectly aligned that it seemed their hearts must be beating in unison. When their bows landed on the final note, they were still looking at each other, even as that note faded into silence.

Somewhere, a single pair of hands was clapping. Then another pair and another, followed by the unmistakable voice of Professor Balboni shouting: "Bravo! Bravo!"

Under the stage lights they embraced, laughing and giddy about their flawless performance. They were still laughing as they carried their instruments down the stairs, so caught up in their triumph that they did not notice how quiet it was in the greenroom, where the other contestants waited.

"Miss Balboni." Mr. Alfieri appeared before

them, his face an icy mask of rage. "You and your companion will leave the building at once."

"Why?" said Laura.

"It's the express orders of the committee."

"But the prize hasn't been announced yet."

"You were not official contestants. You cannot win."

Lorenzo said, "You just heard us. *Everyone* heard our performance. You can't pretend it didn't happen."

"Officially, it did not." Alfieri thrust a sheet of paper in Lorenzo's face. "Here are the new rules, issued yesterday by the committee. Since the September decree, your people may not attend this or any college. Since the competition is sponsored by Ca' Foscari, you were not allowed to compete."

"*I'm* not of the Jewish race," said Laura.

"You too are disqualified, Miss Balboni."

"Simply because my partner is a Jew?"

"That is correct."

"There's not a violinist in this competition who can match him."

"I'm merely following the rules."

"Which you never question."

"They *are* the rules. You violated them and forced your way onstage. This behavior is abominable. You will both leave the building."

"We will not," said Laura.

Alfieri turned to two men who were standing behind him and ordered: "Remove them."

Laura turned to the other contestants, who'd been watching in silence. "We're musicians just like you are! How can this be fair? You know it's wrong!"

One of Alfieri's men grabbed her arm and began dragging her toward the exit.

Enraged by the sight of that rough hand on Laura's flesh, Lorenzo wrenched the man away and shoved him against the wall. "Don't you touch her!"

"Animal!" shouted Mr. Alfieri. "You see, they're all filthy animals!"

An arm came around Lorenzo's throat and as he was hauled backward, a fist slammed into his belly. Laura shrieked for the two men to stop, but they kept pummeling his ribs and he heard the sickening crack of bone. Music stands toppled as they dragged him across the room to the exit.

Heaved out the door, he landed facedown on cold pavement. Felt blood seep from his lip and heard the wheeze of his own lungs as he fought to breathe.

"Oh God. Oh God!" Laura dropped to her knees beside him and he felt her hair, silky and fragrant, fall across his face as she rolled him onto his back. "This is *my* fault. I should never have argued with them! I'm sorry, Lorenzo, I'm so sorry."

"Don't, Laura." Coughing, he sat up and felt the street spin around him. Saw his own blood drip, black as ink, onto his white shirt. "Never apologize for doing what's right."

"I stood up to them, but *you're* the one they punished. I'm so stupid. It's easy for *me* to take a stand, but I'm not a Jew."

The truth of what she said hit him like a fresh

blow, this one straight to his heart. She was not a Jew, and that chasm between them had never seemed wider. He sat with blood dripping down his chin, as warm as tears, and wished Laura would go away. Just go away.

The stage door squealed open and he heard the hesitant approach of footsteps. It was one of the musicians.

"I brought out your instruments," the young man said, gently setting down the cello and violin cases. "I wanted to be sure they were returned to you."

"Thank you," said Laura.

The young man started toward the stage door, then looked back at them. "It's wrong, what they're doing. It's completely unfair. But what can I do? What can *any* of us do?" With a sigh, he walked away.

"Coward," said Laura.

"But he's right." Lorenzo struggled to his feet and for a moment he stood swaying, fighting the dizziness. His head cleared and he saw everything in heartbreaking focus. This was now the way of the world. Laura refused to acknowledge it, but he saw the painful truth.

He picked up his violin. "I'm going home."

"You're hurt." She reached for his arm. "Let me walk with you."

"Don't, Laura." He pushed her hand away. *"Don't."*

"I only want to help!"

"You can't fight my battles. You'll only get hurt."

He gave a bitter laugh. "And you'll probably get *me* killed."

"I didn't know this would happen," she said, her voice breaking. "I really thought we would win tonight."

"We *should* have won. No one can match us on that stage, no one. But I took away any chance you had of winning. I stole that from you, Laura. I won't let that happen again."

"Lorenzo," she said as he walked away, but he did not stop. He kept walking, gripping the violin case so tightly that his fingers went numb. He turned the corner and he could still hear her voice echoing off the buildings, the sound of his name fragmented into desolate shards.

No one was at home when he arrived; they were still at the competition. He peeled off his soiled shirt and washed his face. As bloodied water swirled down the sink drain, he stared in the mirror at a face that had swollen into a purple balloon. *This is what happens when you fight back,* he thought, and Laura had witnessed the whole humiliating spectacle. She'd seen his defeat, his impotence. He bowed his head, hands balled into fists, and spat blood-tinged saliva into the sink.

"So now you understand how the world has changed," said Marco.

Lorenzo looked up at the reflection of his older brother, who stood behind him. "Leave me alone."

"I've been saying it for months, but you didn't listen. Papa, Grandpapa, no one listened. No one believed me."

"Even if we did believe you, what were we supposed to do about it?"

"Fight back."

Lorenzo turned to face Marco. "You think I didn't try?"

Marco snorted. "Hardly. You've been living in a fantasy, Brother. All these months I've pointed out the clues, yet you refused to see any of it. Instead you were wrapped up in your little romantic daydreams. You and Laura Balboni? Do you really think that could ever amount to anything?"

"Shut up."

"Oh, she's pretty, all right. I can see the attraction. Maybe she has a thing for you, too. Maybe you hoped our families would approve and you'd get married."

"Shut up."

"But in case you weren't paying attention, that will soon be illegal. Didn't you see the latest bulletin from the Grand Council? They're writing a new law that forbids mixed marriages. All these changes, and you never noticed it happening. While the world collapsed around us, you mooned over your music and Laura. If you really care about her, you'll forget her. Otherwise, it'll be heartbreak for you both." Marco placed a firm hand on his shoulder. "Be sensible. Forget her."

Lorenzo swiped at tears that suddenly clouded his eyes. He wanted to fling aside Marco's hand, wanted to tell him to go to hell because *sensible* advice was not what he wanted to hear. Yet everything Marco said was true. Laura was beyond his reach. Everything was beyond his reach.

"There's a way out for us," Marco said quietly.

"What do you mean?"

Marco's voice dropped even lower. "We leave Italy. Other families are going. You heard what Balboni said. We should emigrate."

"Papa will never leave."

"Then we have to go without him. Without any of them. They're stuck in the past and they'll never change. But you and I, we could go to Spain together."

"And leave them behind? You would do that, say goodbye to Mama and Pia and not look back?" Lorenzo shook his head. "How can you even consider it?"

"It might come down to that. If we're left with no other choice, if they refuse to see what's about to happen."

"That's not a choice I would ever—" He stopped at the sound of the door slamming shut.

Their sister called out: "Lorenzo? Lorenzo?" Pia ran in and threw her arms around him. "They told us what happened to you! My poor brother, how can they be so mean? Are you hurt badly? Are you going to be all right?"

"I'm fine, little Pia. As long as you're here to take care of me, I'll be just fine." He wrapped his arms around her, and over her bent head he met his brother's gaze. *Look at her, Marco. Would you leave Italy without her?*

Would you leave our sister?

Julia ∽

9

Waiting rooms and more waiting rooms. Since my daughter stabbed me with glass, that's what our lives have come down to: Lily and me, sitting on a series of sofas in doctors' offices, waiting for a nurse to call her name. First we see her pediatrician, Dr. Cherry, who seems a bit put out that he might have missed a serious brain disorder. Then there's an afternoon with Dr. Salazar, the pediatric neurologist, who asks me the same questions I've heard again and again. *Has Lily ever had febrile convulsions? Has she ever fallen and lost consciousness? Has she been in any accidents or hit her head?* No, no, and no. While I'm relieved that no one thinks I'm the one who needs a psychiatrist, now I face a possibility that's even more frightening: that there is something very wrong with my daughter's brain. Something that made her twice go berserk. At only three years old, she has already massacred our cat and stabbed me in the leg. What will she be capable of when she's eighteen?

Dr. Salazar orders a battery of new tests and this leads to our sitting in yet another series of waiting rooms. Lily has X-rays, which come back normal; blood tests, which are also normal; and finally an electroencephalogram.

It is inconclusive.

"EEGs can sometimes miss a lesion, if the abnormal electrical discharges involve only subcortical regions," Dr. Salazar tells me when I visit his office late on a Friday afternoon.

It has been a long day, and I have trouble focusing on what he's telling me. I don't think I'm a stupid woman, but really—what the hell did he just say? Lily is out in the waiting room with Val, and through the closed door I can hear my daughter calling for me, and this distracts me even more. I'm annoyed at Rob for not being here beside me and my head still aches from that bump against the coffee table. Now this doctor won't speak to me in plain English.

He tosses out other words that sound like a foreign language. *Neuro-developmental defects such as heterotopic gray matter. Neuroimaging techniques. Cortical electrical activity. Complex partial seizures.*

That last word leaps out and instantly grips me in its jaws: *seizures.* "Wait," I cut in. "Are you saying Lily might have epilepsy?"

"Although her EEG appears to be normal, there's still the possibility that both incidents were manifestations of a certain type of seizure disorder."

"But she's never convulsed. Not that I've seen."

"I'm not talking about classic tonic-clonic seizures, where you fall unconscious and your limbs shake. No, it's her *behavior* that might be the manifestation of epilepsy. These are what we call complex partial seizures, or CPS. They're often misdiagnosed as psychiatric disorders, because the patients appear to be awake during the seizure, and may even perform complex acts. They'll keep repeating a phrase, for instance. Or they'll walk in circles or tug at their clothes."

"Or stab someone."

He pauses. "Yes. That could be considered a complex repetitive act."

I'm suddenly struck by a memory. Blood running down my leg. The sound of a voice, flat and mechanical. " 'Hurt Mommy,' " I murmur.

"Excuse me?"

"After she stabbed me, she kept saying two words. 'Hurt Mommy,' over and over."

He nodded. "That would certainly count as a repetitive act. Since these patients are completely unaware of their environment, they can get into dangerous situations. They've been known to walk into traffic or fall out of windows. And when the seizure's over, they have no memory of what happened. It's just a gap in time that they can't explain."

"Then she can't control it? She doesn't *mean* to hurt anyone?"

"That's right. Assuming these *are* seizures."

How strange it is to feel so relieved that my daughter might have epilepsy, but that's exactly how I feel right now, because it explains these last terrible weeks. It means Lily can't help what she did. It means she's the same sweet daughter I've always loved, and I don't have to be afraid of her.

"Can this be treated?" I ask. "Is there a cure?"

"Perhaps not a cure, but the seizures can be brought under control, and we have a wide range of anticonvulsant drugs to choose from. But let's not get ahead of ourselves. I'm not yet certain this *is* the cause of her behavior. There's one more test I want to order. It's called a magnetoencephalography, or MEG for short. It records electrical currents in the brain."

"Isn't that what the EEG did?"

"MEG is far more sensitive to lesions the EEG might miss, lesions located deep in the folds of the brain. To do the test, the patient sits in a chair and wears a type of helmet. Even if she moves around a little bit, we can still record the electrical currents. We'll introduce various stimuli and see if that changes her brain activity."

"What kind of stimuli?"

"In your daughter's case, it would be auditory. You said that both times she showed this aggressive behavior, you were playing a particular violin piece. Something with very high-frequency notes."

"You think the music brought on these seizures?"

"Theoretically it's possible. We know seizures can be set off by visual stimuli—blinking lights or repetitive flashes, for instance. Maybe Lily's brain is sensitive to notes at certain frequencies, or in specific combinations. We'll play that piece of music through her headphones while we monitor her brain's electrical activity. See if we can induce the same aggressive behavior."

What he suggests sounds perfectly logical and of course it must be done. But it means someone must record *Incendio,* and I dread the thought of playing those notes. I now associate that waltz with blood, with pain, and I never want to hear it again.

"I'll schedule the MEG for next Wednesday. We'll need a recording of the music before then," he says.

"There isn't any recording. At least—I don't think there is. It's a handwritten composition I bought in an antiques store."

"Then why don't you record yourself playing it? You can email the digital file to me."

"I can't. I mean . . ." I take a deep breath. "I haven't mastered the piece. It's quite demanding. But I can ask my friend Gerda to record it. She plays first violin in our quartet."

"Fine. Ask her to email the file by Tuesday. And bring Lily to the hospital next Wednesday, eight A.M." He smiles as he closes Lily's chart. "I know this has been a rough time for you, Mrs. Ansdell. I hope this test will give us the answer."

10

This time Rob also comes to the doctor's appointment, which for some reason irritates me. In the days leading up to this, I'm the one who's done all the driving, all the waiting, shuttling Lily to doctors' offices and labs. Only now, at the main event, does Rob finally decide to show up. After the MEG technician takes our daughter into the next room to be tested, Rob and I settle onto a hideous plaid-upholstered sofa in the waiting area. Though we're right beside each other, we don't hold hands, we don't even touch. I open one of the women's magazines on the coffee table, but I'm too nervous to read, so I aimlessly flip through glossy images of leather purses and high heels and models with dewdrop-perfect skin.

"At least this is something we can treat," Rob says. "If one anticonvulsant drug doesn't work, there's always another one we can try." He's researched all the drugs, of course. My husband has compiled pages and pages of printouts on epilepsy medicines, their dosages, and their side effects. Now that he has a name for Lily's problem, he's prepared to tackle it like any man of action. "And if none of the drugs work, there are neurosurgical procedures they can try," he adds, as if this is comforting news.

"They haven't even made the diagnosis," I snap. "Don't talk about surgery."

"Okay. Sorry." At last he reaches for my hand. "Are you feeling all right, Julia?"

"I'm not the patient. Why are you asking me?"

"Dr. Cherry told me that when a child's sick, the whole family becomes a patient. I know this has been really tough on you."

"And it hasn't been for you?"

"You've had to bear the brunt of it. You're not sleeping, and you're hardly eating anything these days. Do you think it might help if you talked to someone? Michael recommended this psychiatrist, a woman who specializes in—"

"Wait. You've been talking to the guys at work about me?"

He shrugs. "It just came up in conversation. Michael asked how you and Lily were doing."

"I hope you didn't tell him all the humiliating details." I pull my hand away from his and massage my head, which is aching from this conversation. "So your colleagues now think I need a shrink?"

"Julia." Sighing, he drapes his arm around my shoulder. "Everything will be fine, okay? No matter what happens, whatever the test shows, we'll get through this together."

The door opens and we both look up as Dr. Salazar walks into the waiting room. "Lily is the perfect little patient," he says, smiling. "The tech's keeping her busy with some toys right now, so let's talk about the results." He sits down facing us, and I try to read his expression, but all I see is that bland smile. I have no clue what he's about to tell us. "During the test, we challenged her with a number of different stimuli, both visual and auditory. Flashing lights, different acoustic tones. Loud and soft, high frequency, low. Nothing we tried elicited any seizure activity whatsoever. Her brain appears to process and react in perfectly normal ways."

"You're saying she *doesn't* have epilepsy?" Rob asks.

"Correct. Based on these results, I'd have to say she does not have a seizure disorder."

I feel as if I've been whipped into another turn of the roller coaster. I'd already accepted that epilepsy was the cause of Lily's behavior; now I'm left with no explanation at all, which is even worse than epilepsy because I'm back to my daughter the cat killer, the mom slasher. The monster who chants *hurt Mommy, hurt Mommy* as she plunges broken glass into my leg.

"At this point, I don't see any need for further testing," Dr. Salazar says. "I think Lily is a perfectly normal child."

"But what about her behavior?" I ask. Yes, that pesky little issue that first brought us here.

"Now that we've ruled out neurological abnormalities, it might be appropriate to consult a child psychiatrist," says Dr. Salazar. "She's very young, but her behavior might be significant, even at only three years old."

"And you tried *everything* during the test? Did you play the waltz for her? I know Gerda sent you the recording."

"Yes, we did play it. It's a beautiful piece, by the way, very haunting. We played the entire recording three times, through Lily's headphones. All we saw was some increased electrical activity in the right prefrontal and parietal cortex."

"What does that mean?"

"Those particular regions of the brain are thought to be associated with long-term auditory memory. When you hear something for the first time—a random series of tones, for instance—it stays with you for only a few seconds. But if you hear it repeatedly, or if it's something with personal significance, then it recycles through the hippocampus and the limbic system. It picks up emotional tags and gets stored in the cerebral cortex. Since it's stored in Lily's long-term memory, clearly she's heard this waltz a number of times before."

"But she hasn't." Bewildered, I look back and forth at Rob and Dr. Salazar. "I've only played it for her twice."

"Even in utero, fetuses register voices and music. She probably heard you practicing while you were pregnant."

"I've had the music for only a few weeks."

"Then perhaps she heard it somewhere else. In preschool, maybe?"

"It's an unpublished piece." As my agitation

mounts, both Dr. Salazar and Rob appear maddeningly calm. "I don't know of any recording, anywhere. How could it be in her long-term memory?"

Dr. Salazar reaches across to pat my hand. "This is nothing to get excited about, Mrs. Ansdell," he says in his soothing *I have all the answers* voice. "You're a professional musician, so you probably process sounds in a different way than most people. If I played a new tune for you, I'm sure you'd pick it up right away. Maybe you'd still remember it next month, because your brain's primed to send it straight to long-term memory. It appears you've passed that remarkable skill on to your daughter. Also, there's the fact your husband is mathematically inclined." Dr. Salazar looks at Rob. "Math and musical ability seem to be strongly linked in the brain. Children who learn to read music and play an instrument at an early age are often gifted in math. So your genes probably contributed as well."

"That makes perfect sense to me," Rob says.

"I read a biography of Mozart that said he needed to hear a piece played only once, and he could write it all down. That's true musical talent, and your daughter's clearly wired for it. Just like you are."

But my daughter is *not* like me. While I can hum the first bars of the melody, I have certainly not memorized *Incendio*. Yet in my three-year-old daughter's brain, the waltz has somehow embedded itself as permanent memory. An old memory.

We've got a little Mozart on our hands is the

message that Rob took away from our visit with Dr. Salazar, and he's smiling as we drive home. Instead of a daughter with epilepsy, it turns out we have a golden-haired musical genius. He's forgotten about the reason why she had the brain test to begin with, and how this cycle of doctor visits and X-rays and EEGs all began. He doesn't have the painful reminders that still plague me: the dull headache that persists after my fall against the coffee table. The healing laceration on my thigh that still throbs even though the stitches have been removed. He's already moved on to thinking about his genius daughter, and has skipped past the question that no one has answered: Why did my daughter attack me?

By the time we arrive home, Lily's fallen asleep and she doesn't stir as Rob lifts her from her car seat and carries her upstairs to her room. I'm exhausted as well, and after Rob leaves to go back to work, I stretch out on our bed for a nap. But when I close my eyes, all I see is Lily's face, which looks so much like my own.

And so much like my mother's. The mother I don't remember. The mother no one ever wants to talk about.

According to aunt Val, my mother was a gifted musician who sang and played the piano. My father was certainly no musician. He sang off-key, couldn't read a note, couldn't keep a beat. If musical talent is something you inherit, then mine came from my mother, and through me, those genes were passed to Lily. What else did I unwittingly pass on to my daughter?

When I awaken from my nap, I find the sun has already fallen behind the trees and the room is cast in shadow. How long have I slept? I know Rob is home from work, because I hear a kitchen cabinet thump shut downstairs. He must have found me still asleep and decided to start cooking dinner.

Groggy, I climb out of bed and yell from the doorway: "Rob, I have pork chops defrosting in the refrigerator. Did you find them?"

Downstairs, a pot lid clatters.

Yawning, I shuffle to the stairway and call down: "I'm up now. I can take over. You really don't have to—"

My foot suddenly shoots out from under me. I try to catch myself on the railing, but a chasm seems to open up beneath me and I tumble into its jaws, falling, sliding.

When I open my eyes, I'm lying at the bottom of the stairs. I can move my arms and legs, but when I try to turn onto my side, pain stabs my right flank, sharp as a spear. Sobbing, I collapse flat on my back and feel something roll away from my foot and skitter across the wood floor. It's something small and pink and it collides with the wall a few feet away.

A little plastic car. A toy.

"Rob!" I cry out. Surely he heard me tumble down the stairs. Why doesn't he answer? Why doesn't he come out of the kitchen? "Help. Rob, help me . . ."

But it's not Rob who comes out of the kitchen.

Lily crosses to the toy car, picks it up, and examines it with the detached gaze of a scientist studying some failed experiment.

"It was you," I whisper. "You did it."

She looks at me. "Time to get up, Mommy," she says, and walks back into the kitchen.

11

"She did it on purpose. She placed that toy car on the second step, where I'd be sure to slip on it. Then she made noises in the kitchen, to wake me up and draw me downstairs. She *wanted* this to happen."

My husband is trying his best to maintain a neutral expression. He sits by our bed, where I lie propped up on pillows and groggy from Vicodin. I've broken no bones but my back is knotted in pain and I can barely move without sending my muscles into fresh spasms. He doesn't look at me, but stays focused on the duvet, as if he can't bring himself to meet my gaze. I know how absurd I sound, claiming that a three-year-old plotted to kill me, but the pain pills have loosened all the connections in my brain, and a whole host of possibilities floats around me, like poisonous gnats.

Lily is downstairs with my aunt Val, and I hear her call out: "Mommy? Mommy, come play with us!" My darling daughter. I shudder at the sound of her voice.

Rob lets out a troubled sigh. "I'm going to make an appointment for you, Julia. This doctor comes highly recommended. I think she can help you."

"I don't want to see a psychiatrist."

"You need to see *someone*."

"Our daughter is trying to *kill* me. I'm not the one who needs therapy."

"She's not trying to kill you. She's only three years old."

"You weren't here, Rob. You didn't see her studying that toy car, as if trying to understand why it didn't work. Why it didn't kill me."

"Can't you hear her calling for you right now? That's our baby, and she wants you. She loves you."

"There's something wrong with her. She's changed. She's not the same baby anymore."

He moves onto the bed and takes my hand. "Julia, remember the day she was born? Remember how you cried because you were so happy? You kept saying how perfect she was, and you wouldn't let the nurse take her away because you couldn't stand not being with her."

I bow my head to hide the tears sliding down my cheeks. Yes, I remember weeping with joy. I remember thinking that I would willingly throw myself off a cliff to keep my baby safe.

He strokes my hair. "She's still our little girl, Julia, and you love her. I know you do."

"She's not the same girl. She's turned into someone else. *Something* else."

"It's the pain pills talking. Why don't you go to sleep now? When you wake up, you'll wonder why you said all these crazy things."

"She's not my baby. She's been different ever since . . ." I lift my head as the memory takes shape through my Vicodin haze. A warm and muggy afternoon. Lily sitting on the patio. My bow gliding across the violin strings.

That's when everything changed. That's when the nightmare began, when I first played *Incendio*.

My friend Gerda lives at the end of a quiet lane in the suburb of Milton, just outside Boston. As I pull into her driveway, I spot her straw hat bobbing among the flowery jungle of delphiniums and when she sees me, she rises easily to her feet. At sixty-five, silver-haired Gerda's still as nimble as a teenager. *Maybe I should take up yoga, too,* I think as I watch her stride toward me, peeling off her garden gloves. I'm half her age, but my stiff back makes me feel like an old woman today.

"Sorry I'm late," I say. "I had to stop at the post office, and the line went out the door."

"Well, you're here now, and that's what matters. Come in, I've made fresh lemonade."

We step into her cluttered kitchen, where bundles of fragrant herbs hang from the ceiling beam. Perched on her refrigerator is an old bird's nest she found abandoned somewhere, and on the windowsill is her dusty collection of seashells and river stones. Rob would call this place a housekeeping emergency, but I find all these messy, eccentric touches strangely comforting.

Gerda takes the pitcher of lemonade out of the refrigerator. "Did you bring that letter from the shopkeeper?"

I reach into my shoulder bag and pull out the envelope. "It was mailed ten days ago, from Rome. His granddaughter wrote it."

As I sip lemonade, Gerda slips on her eyeglasses and reads the letter aloud.

Dear Mrs. Ansdell,

I am writing on behalf of my grandfather Stefano Padrone, who cannot speak English. I showed him the photocopies you sent, and he remembers selling you the music. He says he acquired the book of Gypsy tunes quite a few years ago, along with other items, from the estate of a man named Giovanni Capobianco, who lived in the town of Casperia. He does not have any information about "Incendio" but he will ask the Capobianco family if they know the composer or where it came from.

Sincerely, Anna Maria Padrone

"I haven't heard anything new since I received that letter," I tell Gerda. "I've called the antiques store three times and left messages. No one answers the phone."

"Maybe he's on vacation. Maybe he hasn't had a chance to talk to the family." She rises to her feet. "Come on, let's take another look at that waltz."

We go into her cluttered practice room, where a baby grand piano leaves barely enough space for a bookcase, two chairs, and a coffee table. Stacks of sheet music are piled high on the floor like stalagmites in a cave. On her music stand is the copy of *Incendio* that I scanned and emailed to her three weeks ago, when she recorded the piece for Lily's neurological test. It's merely two sheets of paper dotted with notes, but I feel its power. As if, at any instant, it could glow red or levitate.

"This is a gorgeous waltz, but it's definitely challenging," says Gerda, settling down in front of the music stand. "It took me a few hours of practice to get the arpeggios under my fingers and to hit these high notes just right."

"I never did manage it," I admit, feeling as if I've just confirmed every bad joke ever told about second violin players. *Question: How many second violinists does it take to screw in a lightbulb? Answer: They can't go that high.*

Gerda takes her violin out of the case. "The trick to this passage here is to make the shift to fifth position a measure earlier." She demonstrates, and her notes scamper up the E string at a blistering speed.

"You don't need to play it now," I cut in.

"It really does make this next section easier to manage. Listen."

"Please *stop*." Even I am shocked by how shrill my voice sounds. I take a deep breath and say quietly: "Just tell me what you've found out about the waltz."

Frowning, Gerda sets down her violin. "What's the matter?"

"I'm sorry. It gives me a headache listening to it. Can we just talk about the music?"

"All right. But first, can I look at the original?"

I open my shoulder bag, take out the book of printed Gypsy music, and flip it open to where I've tucked in the loose sheet with *Incendio*. I'm reluctant to even touch the sheet, so I simply hand Gerda the whole book.

She pulls out the waltz and examines the yellowed page, both front and back. "Written in pencil. Standard manuscript paper, looks pretty brittle. I don't see any watermark, and there's nothing to identify its origin except the title and the composer's name, L. Todesco." She glances up at me. "I looked up that name online and I can't find any published music by this composer." She squints more closely at the page. "Okay, this is interesting. On the other side, there are a number of partly erased notes, which were then written over. It looks like these four measures were revised."

"So he wasn't just copying the music straight from another source."

"No, these changes are too extensive to be a simple transcription error. This must be the actual page he composed it on. And then he made these changes." She glances at me over her glasses. "You know, this could be the only copy of the piece in existence. Since it's never been recorded."

"How do you know there's no recording?"

"Because I sent a copy over to Paul Frohlich at the conservatory. He ran it through all his music recognition programs, comparing it to every known recorded piece. There are no matches anywhere. As far as he can tell, this waltz was never recorded, and he can't find any published music under the name L. Todesco. So we're completely in the dark about where the waltz comes from."

"What about the book of Gypsy tunes? I found *Incendio* tucked inside it, so maybe they came from the same owner. Maybe the book belonged to this L. Todesco."

She opens the fragile collection of melodies. The cover is crisscrossed with brittle Scotch tape, which seems to be the only thing holding it together. Gently she turns to the copyright page. "It's an Italian publisher. Printed in 1921."

"There's something written on the back cover."

Gerda flips over the book and sees the faded words, handwritten in blue ink: *11 Calle del Forno, Venezia.* "That's an address in Venice."

"Maybe the composer's address?"

"That would certainly be a starting point for our search. We should compile a list of everyone who's lived at that address since 1921." She turns her attention back to the two pages of music on her stand. "*Incendio.* Fire. I wonder what kind of fire the title refers to." She picks up her instrument, and before I can stop her, she starts to play. As the first notes ring from her violin, I feel a rising sense of panic. My hands begin to tingle, an electrical current that builds with each note, until it seems my nerves are screaming. I'm about to snatch the bow away from her when she abruptly stops playing and stares at the music.

"Love," she murmurs.

"What?"

"Don't you hear it? The passion, the anguish in this music. In these first sixteen bars, where the melody's introduced, such sadness and longing. Then at measure seventeen, it grows agitated. The pitch climbs and the notes speed up. I can almost imagine two frantic lovers growing desperate." Gerda looks at me. "*Incendio*. I think it's the fire of love."

"Or hell," I say softly, and rub my temples. "Please don't play it anymore. I don't think I can stand hearing it."

She sets down the violin. "This isn't just about the music, is it? What's really going on, Julia?"

"It *is* about the music."

"Lately you've been so distracted. You've missed two quartet rehearsals in a row." She pauses. "Is there something wrong between you and Rob?"

I don't know what to tell her, so for a moment I don't say a thing. It's so quiet here in Gerda's home. She lives alone, with no husband, no children; she has to answer only to herself, while I'm forced to share a house with a man who questions my sanity and a daughter who scares me.

"It has to do with Lily," I finally admit. "She's been having problems."

"What problems?"

"Remember when I told you I cut my leg and needed stitches?"

"You said it was an accident."

"It wasn't an accident." I look at her. "Lily did it."

"What do you mean?"

"She pulled a piece of broken glass out of the trash can. And she stabbed me with it."

Gerda stares. "*Lily* did that?"

I wipe away tears. "And that day I fell, that wasn't an accident, either. She left a toy on the stairs, right where I'd step on it. No one believes me, but I know she did it on purpose." I take a few breaths and at last manage to regain control. When I speak again, my voice is flat. Defeated. "I don't know who she is anymore. She's turned into someone else. I look at her and I see a stranger, someone who wants to hurt me. And it all started when I played the waltz."

Anyone else would tell me that I'm delusional, but Gerda says nothing. She just listens, her silence calming and nonjudgmental.

"We took her in for medical tests, and she had a sort of EEG, to look at her brain waves. When they played the waltz for her, her brain responded as if it were a long-term memory. As if she already *knew* this music. Yet you say the waltz has never been recorded."

"An old memory," Gerda murmurs and stares at *Incendio,* as if seeing something in that music that she had missed before. "Julia, I know this is going to sound bizarre," she says softly. "But when I was a child, I had memories that I couldn't possibly explain. My parents put it down to an active imagination, but I remembered a stone hut with a dirt floor. Fields of wheat, waving in the sunlight. And I had a vivid memory of seeing my own bare feet, but with one toe missing. None of it made any sense, until my grandmother told me they were leftover memories of who I once was. In a previous lifetime." She looks at me. "Do you think that's crazy?"

I shake my head. "Nothing seems crazy to me anymore."

"My grandmother said most people don't remember their past lives. Or they refuse to accept those memories as anything but fantasies. But with very young children, their minds are still open. They still have access to prior memories, even if they don't have the language to talk to us about them. Maybe that's why Lily reacts to this waltz. Because she's heard it before, in another lifetime."

I can imagine what Rob would say if he heard this conversation. Already he suspects I'm unbalanced; if I start talking about past lives, he'll have no doubt of it.

"I wish I could offer you some sort of solution to your problem," she says.

"I don't think there is a solution."

"Now I'm *really* curious about this music. If your antiques dealer in Rome can't help us, maybe we can track down the composer ourselves. I'm scheduled to perform at that festival in Trieste, and that's really close to Venice. I could make a quick side trip to the address on Calle del Forno. Find out if L. Todesco ever lived there."

"You'd go to all that trouble for me?"

"It's definitely worth my time, and it wouldn't be just for you. This waltz is gorgeous, and I don't think it's ever been published. What if our quartet could be the first to ever record it? We need to make sure the rights to this waltz are free and clear.

So you see, I have my own selfish reason to track down L. Todesco."

"He's probably long dead."

"Probably." Gerda casts a covetous look at the music. "But what if he isn't?"

When I arrive home after my visit to Gerda, I see Val's Ford Taurus parked in our driveway and Rob's Lexus is already in the garage. I don't know why Rob is home so early, or why they're both standing at the front door when I walk into the house. All I know is that neither one of them is smiling.

"Where the hell have you been?" Rob demands.

"I went to see Gerda. I told you I was going to visit her."

"Do you have any idea what time it is?"

"Was I supposed to be home earlier? I don't remember talking about it."

"Jesus, Julia. What is *wrong* with you?"

My aunt interjects: "Rob, I'm sure she got busy and just lost track of time. There's no need to get mad about it."

"No need? I was about to call the police!"

I shake my head, baffled by this conversation. "Why on earth would you call the police? What have I done?"

"We've both been trying to reach you for hours. When you didn't show up at the preschool, they called me at work. Val had to rush over there and pick up Lily."

"But I've had the phone with me all day. No one's tried to call me."

"We *did* call you, Julia," says Val. "It kept going to voice mail."

"Then something must be wrong with it." I dig the cellphone out of my shoulder bag and stare in dismay at the screen. There they are, all the missed calls and voice mails. From the preschool, from Rob, from Val. "It must be the ringer," I say. "Maybe I accidentally turned it off. Or something's gone wrong with the settings."

"Julia, are you still taking the Vicodin?" Val asks quietly.

"No. No, I stopped it days ago," I mutter as I fumble through the phone menu, trying to find out how I accidentally muted the ringer. My fingers feel clumsy and I keep tapping the wrong icons. I have had nightmares just like this, when I am frantically trying to call for help and I keep dialing the wrong numbers. But this is not a nightmare. This is really happening.

"Stop," Rob says. "Julia, stop."

"No, I need to fix this *now*." I keep tapping through phone menus, even as Lily runs into the hallway, even as her arms encircle my leg like smothering vines.

"Mommy! I miss you, Mommy!"

I look down and in her eyes I suddenly glimpse something poisonous, something that ripples like a serpent to the surface of those still waters and dives once again out of sight. I jerk away from her so sharply that she gives an anguished wail and stands with imploring arms, a child abandoned by her mother.

Val quickly takes my daughter's hand. "Lily, why don't you come stay with me for a few days? I could really use some help picking tomatoes. Mommy and Daddy won't mind if I steal you away, will they?"

Rob gives a weary nod. "I think that'd be a very good idea. Thank you, Val."

"Lily, let's go upstairs and pack a suitcase, okay? You tell me what you want to bring to my house."

"Donkey. I want Donkey."

"Of course, we'll bring Donkey. What about some other toys? And what do you think of spaghetti tonight?"

As Val takes Lily upstairs, Rob and I remain in the foyer. I'm afraid to look at him, afraid to read, in his face, what he thinks of me.

"Julia," he sighs. "Let's go sit down." He takes my arm and leads me into the living room.

"There's something wrong with this goddamn cellphone," I insist.

"I'll take a look at it later, okay? I'll figure it out." That's always been Rob's role in our family. He's the fixer. He checks under the hood and tests wires and finds a solution to every problem. He sits me down on the sofa and sinks into the chair across from me. "Look, I know you're under a lot of stress. You're losing weight. You're not sleeping well."

"I'm still having back pain; that's what's keeping me up. You wanted me to go off the Vicodin, and that's what I did."

"Sweetheart, Val and I both think you need to talk to someone. Please don't think of it as therapy. It'll just be a conversation between you and Dr. Rose."

"Dr. Rose? Is this the psychiatrist you told me about?"

"She comes highly recommended. I've gone over her qualifications. I've looked into her background, her physician ratings."

Of course he has.

"I think she could help you a lot. She could help our whole family. Guide us back to the way we were before all this happened."

"Rob?" Val calls out from upstairs. "Where can I find a suitcase for Lily's stuff?"

"I'll get you one," Rob answers. He pats my hand. "I'll be right back, okay?" he says and heads upstairs to find a suitcase.

I hear him moving around in our bedroom, and then the sound of suitcase wheels rolling across the wood floor. I focus on the living room window, which faces west. Only now do I register how low the sun is in the sky, far too low for three o'clock in the afternoon. No wonder my back is aching again; my last dose of Tylenol was far too many hours ago.

I go into the downstairs bathroom, open the medicine cabinet, and shake out three extra-strength caplets. As the cabinet door swings shut again, I'm startled by my reflection in the mirror. I see uncombed hair, puffy eyes, washed-out skin. I splash cold water on my face and run fingers through my hair, but I still look all wrong. The strain of dealing with Lily has turned me into a ghost of myself. This is the dark side of motherhood that no ever warns you about, the part that's not all hugs and kisses. They don't tell you that the child you once nurtured in your womb, the child you thought would bring you such love, instead begins to gnaw at your soul like a little parasite. I stare at myself and think: *Soon there'll be nothing left of me.*

When I emerge from the bathroom, Rob and Val are back downstairs in the foyer, right around the corner from me. They're talking so softly I can barely hear them, so I move closer.

"Camilla was the same age as Julia is now. That's got to be significant."

"Julia's nothing like her," Val says.

"Still, the genetics are there. Her family history of mental illness."

"Trust me, this is *not* the same situation. Camilla was a cold-blooded psychopath. She was self-centered and clever and manipulative. But she was *not* insane."

They're talking about my mother. My dead, baby-killing mother. I'm desperate to hear every word, but my heart pounds so hard it threatens to drown out their voices.

"All the psychiatrists who saw her agreed," says Rob. "They said she had a psychotic break, lost all touch with reality. These things do run in families."

"She had them fooled, every single one of them. She wasn't psychotic. She was *evil.*"

"Mommy, hold me! Hold me!"

I whirl around to see Lily standing right behind

me. My daughter has exposed me. She looks up at me with perfectly innocent eyes as Val and Rob come around the corner

"Oh there you are!" says Val, trying to sound casual but not quite hitting the right note. "Lily and I are just about to leave. Don't you worry about a thing."

As Lily clings to me in a goodbye hug, I can feel Rob watching me for signs that I'm a danger to my daughter. I know that's what worries him, because he brought up my mother's name, a name that's never spoken in my presence. Until he said it, it hadn't even occurred to me that I'm the same age my mother was when she committed the most unforgivable sin a woman can commit. I wonder if some twisted remnant of her is now stirring to life inside me.

Is this what she felt in the days before she killed my brother? Did she look at her own child and see a monster staring back?

Lorenzo ❧

12

From the back room of his father's luthier shop, Lorenzo heard the tinkle of the bell on the door and he called out: "If you can wait just a minute, I'll be right out to help you."

No one answered.

He had just applied glue and was now clamping the violin's belly to the ribs. This was a delicate step, one he could not rush, and he took care tightening the clamp and confirming the angles. When he finally emerged from the back room, he saw his customer crouched before the display case of cello and viola bows. Only the top of her hat was visible above the counter.

"May I help you?" he asked.

She rose to her feet and smiled at him. "Lorenzo," she said.

Five years had passed since they'd last spoken to each other. Although he'd glimpsed her several times on the street, it had always been from a distance, and he had never approached her. Now he and Laura Balboni stood face-to-face, with only the display case between them, and he could not think of a single thing to say. Her blond hair was short now, cut in the stylish bob that was so popular among female students at Ca' Foscari. Her face had lost its girlish roundness, and her cheekbones were more prominent, her jaw more sharply defined. Her gaze was as direct as ever, so direct that he felt pierced to the spot, unable to move, to say a single word.

"It needs to be rehaired," she said.

He looked down at the cello bow that she'd set on the countertop. The frog end was scraggly with broken horse hairs. "Of course, I'll be happy to do this for you. When will you need it back?"

"There's no rush. I have another bow I can use in the meantime."

"Will next week be soon enough?"

"That would be fine."

"Then you can pick it up on Wednesday."

"Thank you." She lingered for a moment, searching for something more to say. With a sigh of resignation she went to the door. There she stopped and turned back to him. "Is that all we have to say to each other? *Pick it up on Wednesday. Thank you?*"

"You look wonderful, Laura," he said softly. And she did; she was even more beautiful than he remembered, as if the passage of five years had burnished her hair and face into this shimmering version of the seventeen-year-old girl he'd once known. In the gloom of the shop, she seemed to shine with her own light.

"Why haven't you come to see us?" she asked.

He looked around the room and gave an apologetic shrug. "My father needs my help here. And I teach the violin. I have ten students now."

"I sent you half a dozen invitations, Lorenzo. You never came. Not even to my birthday party."

"I did write to you with my regrets."

"Yes, and all your notes were *so* polite. You could have come to tell me in person. Or just stopped in to say hello."

"You were off to study at Ca' Foscari. You have new friends now."

"Which means I can't keep my old ones?"

He stared down at her bow, its frog end bristling with broken hairs. He remembered how vigorously she attacked the cello strings with that bow. No timid strokes for her. A player as fierce as Laura would quickly snap strings and wear out bow hairs. Passion had its price.

"That night, at the competition," he said quietly, "everything changed for us."

"No, it didn't."

"For *you* it didn't." Suddenly angry at her obliviousness, he looked straight at her. "For me, and for my family, *everything* has changed. But not for you. You're allowed to study at Ca' Foscari. You have your new friends, your pretty haircut. Your life goes on, happy and perfect. But mine?" He looked around the shop and gave a bitter laugh. "I'm trapped. Do you think I'm here in this shop because I *choose* to be?"

"Lorenzo," she murmured. "I'm so sorry."

"Come back for your bow on Wednesday. It will be ready."

"I'm not blind. I know what's going on."

"Then you also know why I stay away from you."

"Is it to hide? To keep your head down and stay out of trouble?" She leaned in, confronting him across the countertop. "*Now* is the time to be brave. I want to stand with you. No matter what happens, I want to—" She stopped as the doorbell tinkled.

A customer walked in, a thin-lipped woman who merely nodded to them, then slowly circled the shop, eyeing the violins and violas hanging on the walls. Lorenzo had never seen this woman before and her sudden appearance made him uneasy. His father's luthier business survived only because of a small but devoted clientele. New customers almost never came through the door, but favored the luthier shop down the street, where the words *Negozio Ariano* were so prominently displayed in the window. *Aryan Store.*

Laura seemed to share his uneasiness. Avoiding the woman's gaze, she quickly turned away and proceeded to rummage in her purse.

"Might I assist you, madam?" Lorenzo asked the woman.

"Are you the proprietor of this shop?"

"My father is. I'm his assistant."

"And where is your father?"

"He went home for lunch but he should be back soon. Perhaps there's something I can help you with?"

"No, nothing." The woman looked around at the instruments and her upper lip curled in distaste.

"I simply wondered why anyone would choose to patronize this business."

"Maybe you should ask a musician," Laura said. "Since I assume you're not one."

The woman turned to her. "Excuse me?"

"The finest violins made in Venice come from this luthier shop."

The woman's eyes narrowed. "You're Professor Balboni's daughter, are you not? I saw you perform last month, at La Fenice. Your quartet was excellent."

"I'll tell them," Laura said coolly. She looked at Lorenzo. "I'll be back to pick up my bow on Wednesday."

"Miss Balboni?" the woman called as Laura opened the door to leave. "You really should take a look at Mr. Landra's shop, down the road. He makes very fine instruments." It was not merely a suggestion; there was the dark note of warning in her voice.

Laura glanced back, a retort on her lips, but she said nothing as she walked out. She closed the door so hard that the bell gave a sharp clink.

The woman followed her out of the shop.

Lorenzo could not hear what was said between them, but through the window he saw the woman stop Laura on the street. Saw Laura give a contemptuous shake of her head and storm away. And he thought: *How I've missed you. After five long years, we finally speak again, only to have it end on such a bitter note.*

He picked up Laura's bow from the countertop. Only then did he see the folded piece of paper, which she had tucked under the frog. It had not been there earlier; she must have slipped it under the bow while he and the woman were talking. He unfolded the paper and saw what Laura had written.

My house, tonight. Tell no one.

As instructed, Lorenzo told no one. He said nothing about it when his father returned to the shop after lunch, nor did he speak of it that evening, when his family gathered at the supper table for bread and fish soup, a meal cobbled together from discarded scraps that Marco had brought home from his job hauling crates at the market. It was a hard and dirty job that Marco was lucky to have, thanks to the fishmonger's blatant disregard for the laws against hiring Jews. Throughout Italy, thousands of employers like the fishmonger continued to conduct business as usual, scornful of the new laws, willing to slip young men like Marco a bundle of lire for a hard day's work. Five years ago, how different the future had seemed for Marco, who had dreamed of a career as a diplomat. Now he sat slumped and exhausted at the supper table, smelling of sweat and the permanent stink of fish. Even fiery Marco had been defeated.

The years had beaten down Papa as well. Bruno's clientele had dwindled to only a few customers a week, none of them in the market for a new violin. They purchased only necessities like rosin and strings, which hardly justified keeping the shop open, but six days a week, Bruno would be at his worktable stubbornly carving and sanding and varnishing yet another fine instrument that he could not sell. And when his dwindling supply of seasoned maple and spruce was used up, what then? Would he sit idle in his shop month after month, year after year, until he dried up and crumbled into dust?

The years have changed us all, thought Lorenzo. His mother looked gray and tired, and no wonder. Since her father Alberto's stroke four months ago, Eloisa spent every day at the nursing home spooning food into his mouth, rubbing his back, reading him books and newspapers. Alberto's chair sat empty and waiting for his return home, but that seemed less likely with every passing week. Certainly there would be no more grandfather-grandson violin duets, no more shared tunes and musical games. Alberto could not even control a fork, much less a violin bow.

Of them all, Pia was the only one whom the years had not diminished. She was blossoming into a slender, dark-eyed beauty who would someday catch many a boy's eye, but at fourteen she was too timid to flaunt that beauty. With the schools now closed to her, she spent most of the week helping Mama with Alberto, or reading alone in her room, or daydreaming at the window—about her future husband, no doubt. That much about Pia had not changed; she was still the romantic, still in love with love. *If only I can keep her this way,* thought Lorenzo, *protected from the world as it really is. If only I can keep us all just the way we are right now, together and warm and safe.*

"You're so quiet. Are you all right, Lorenzo?" Pia asked. Of course she would be the one to notice that something was different; with just a glance, she always knew if her brother was tired or troubled or feverish.

He smiled. "Everything is fine."

"Are you sure?"

"He just said he's fine," grumbled Marco. "He didn't have to haul crates of fish all day."

"He *does* work. He has students who pay him."

"Fewer and fewer."

"Marco," warned Eloisa. "We all do our part."

"Except me," Pia sighed. "What do I do except mend a few shirts?"

Lorenzo patted her on the cheek. "You make us all happy just by being yourself."

"A lot of good that does."

"It makes all the difference, Pia."

Because you keep us hopeful, he thought, watching his sister climb the stairs to bed. Marco had left the table with little more than a grunt, but Pia hummed her way up the stairs, an old Gypsy tune that Alberto had taught them when they were children. Pia still believed there was good in everyone. *If only that were true.*

It was well after midnight when Lorenzo slipped out of his house. The December chill had driven most people indoors and a strange mist hung in the air, a mist that stank of fish and sewage. Seldom did he venture out this late at night, for fear of encountering the thuggish Blackshirts who regularly roamed the streets. Two weeks ago Marco had stumbled home covered in blood, his nose broken, his shirt ripped to tatters by just such an encounter.

It could have been far worse.

Lorenzo kept to the shadows, slipping quickly through the smaller alleys, avoiding the lamplit piazzas. At the footbridge into Dorsoduro he hesitated, because crossing the canal would put him out in the open, with no place to hide. But this night was too cold and miserable for even the Blackshirts to venture out in, and he saw no one. Head down, his face buried in his scarf, he crossed the footbridge and made his way to Laura.

These last five years, the grand house on Fondamenta Bragadin had called to him like a siren's song, tempting him with a possible glimpse of her. Again and again he'd found himself standing on this same footbridge, lured toward the street he'd so happily walked on before. Once, he could not even remember how he'd arrived at the bridge; his feet had simply carried him there of their own accord. He was like a horse that knows its way home and will always turn toward it.

Outside her house he paused, looking up at windows that on earlier visits had blazed with light. Tonight the house seemed far less welcoming, the curtains tightly drawn, the rooms dimly lit. He swung the brass knocker and felt the wood tremble like something alive.

All at once there she was, backlit in the doorway, her hand grasping his. "Quickly," she whispered, pulling him inside.

The instant he stepped across the threshold, she closed and latched the door behind him. Even in the dim alcove he could see her cheeks were flushed, her eyes electric.

"Thank God you made it here. Papa and I have been so worried."

"What is this all about?"

"We thought there was still plenty of time to arrange things. But after that woman came into your shop today, I knew there *was* no time left."

He followed her down the hallway to the dining room, where he'd enjoyed such happy evenings with the Balbonis. He remembered laughter and countless glasses of wine and talk of music, always music. Tonight he found the table empty, with not even a bowl of fruit. Only one small lamp was burning, and the windows facing the garden were tightly shuttered.

Professor Balboni sat in his usual chair at the head of the table, but this was not the dapper, cheerful gentleman Lorenzo remembered. This was a somber, weary version, so different that Lorenzo could scarcely believe he was the same man.

Balboni mustered a semblance of a smile as he rose to greet their guest. "Fetch the wine, Laura!" he said. "Let's have a toast to our long-lost violinist."

Laura set three goblets and a bottle on the table, but as Balboni poured, the mood in the room was far from celebratory; no, there was a grimness to his face, as if this precious bottle might be the last they would ever enjoy together.

"*Salute,*" said Balboni. He drank without pleasure, set down his empty glass, and looked at Lorenzo. "You were not followed here?"

"No."

"You're certain?"

"I saw no one." Lorenzo looked at Laura, then back at her father. "It's going to happen in Venice, isn't it? The same thing that happened in Rome."

"It will come more quickly than I expected. The armistice changed everything and now we sit in occupied Italy. The SS is solidifying control, and what they did to Jews last month in Rome, they'll do here. Professor Jona predicted this would happen. That's why he burned the community documents, so the SS wouldn't have any of your names. He sacrificed himself to give everyone precious time to escape, yet your family is still here. Your father refuses to see the coming catastrophe, and he puts you all in danger."

"It's not just Papa who keeps us here," said Lorenzo. "Since my grandfather's stroke, he can't even walk. How can he leave the convalescent home? Mama will never leave without him."

A look of pain crossed Balboni's face. "Your grandfather is one of my dearest friends. You know that. It breaks my heart to say this, but there's no hope for him. Alberto is lost, and there's nothing you can do to change that."

"And you say you're his *friend*?"

"I say this *especially* as his friend. Because I know he would want you to be safe, and it's no longer safe in Venice. Surely you've noticed how many of your violin students have stopped coming to lessons? How many of your neighbors have quietly left their homes? Just vanished without notice, telling no one where they've gone. They've heard what happened in Rome. A thousand people rounded up and deported. The same thing is happening in Trieste and Genoa."

"This is *Venice*. Papa says it won't happen here."

"Even as we speak, the SS is compiling the names and addresses of every Jew in the city. They had a brief setback when Professor Jona burned all those documents, but your time has run out. That woman who came to your shop today, she's almost certainly one of them. She was there to survey what's to be confiscated. Under the November Manifesto, all property owned by Jews can be seized. The house, your father's shop, none of it belongs to you, and they will take it any day now."

"This is what Marco has been saying all along."

"Your brother understands. He knows what's about to happen."

"How do *you* know this is going to happen? How can you be so certain?"

"Because I told him so," a voice said behind Lorenzo.

He turned to see the Balbonis' housekeeper, Alda, the sour-faced gargoyle who always seemed to be lurking in the background. Five years ago, she had warned Lorenzo not to take part in the competition and had hinted darkly of the consequences.

He turned to Balboni. "You trust *her*? She's a Blackshirt!"

"No, Lorenzo. She's not."

"She knew what would happen at the competition."

"And I tried to warn you, but you refused to lis-

ten," said Alda. "You're lucky you got off with
only a beating that night."

"Alda's not a Blackshirt, but she does have connections," said Balboni. "She hears things, about
what the SS is planning. We've warned as many
Jews as we can, but not everyone listens. Your father being one of them."

"The idiot," the housekeeper muttered.

Balboni shook his head. "Alda."

"He doesn't believe because he refuses to believe."

"And who can blame him? Who can believe the
SS would dismember a family in Intra? Massacre
children at Lago Maggiore? Everyone thinks
they're just tall tales to make Jews flee the country."

"That's what Papa thinks," said Lorenzo.

"Which is why it's impossible to save Bruno. But
we can save you, and perhaps your sister and
brother as well."

"There's no time to waste," Laura said urgently.
"By tomorrow night, you must be gone. Pack only
what you can carry."

"Where are we to go? Do we hide here?"

"No, this house is not safe," said Professor Balboni. "My sympathies are too well-known, and I
fear they'll search us. But there is a monastery outside Padua where you can stay for a few days. The
monks will keep you hidden until we can find
someone to guide you to the Swiss border." He
placed a hand on Lorenzo's shoulder. "Have faith,
son. Everywhere in Italy, you'll find friends. The

challenge is knowing which people you can trust. And which you cannot."

Everything was happening too fast. Lorenzo knew that Marco would agree to leave, but how could he convince his sister? And Mama would never abandon her father, Alberto, in the convalescent home. He dreaded the wailing and arguments to come, the heartbreak and the guilt. Overwhelmed by what he would have to do next, he drew in a deep breath and steadied himself against the table.

"So I must leave them to the SS. My mother and father."

"I'm afraid you have no other choice."

Lorenzo turned to Laura. "Could you leave *your* father behind? Knowing you might never see him again?"

Her eyes suddenly shimmered with tears. "It's a terrible choice, Lorenzo. But you have to save yourself."

"Could you do it, Laura?"

She wiped a hand across her eyes and looked away. "I don't know."

"I would want her to make that choice," said Professor Balboni. "In fact, I would *insist* on it. These last few weeks have been deceptively quiet. That's why your father believes you can all survive by simply keeping your heads down and making no fuss. But time *is* running out and the arrests will soon start. I'm telling you this because I owe it to my friend Alberto, and because you have a musical gift that should be shared with the world. But the world will never hear you play if you don't survive this war."

"Listen to Papa," said Laura. "Please."

Someone pounded on the front door, and they all snapped to attention. Laura shot her father a look of panic.

"Take him upstairs. Go," Balboni whispered. "Alda, clear away the wineglasses. We want no sign that we've had a visitor."

Laura grabbed Lorenzo's hand and led him to the back stairs. As they scurried up to the second floor, they heard more pounding on the front door. Heard Balboni call out: "What's all the fuss, is the house burning down? I'm coming, I'm coming!"

Laura and Lorenzo slipped into a bedroom and pressed their ears to the closed door, straining to hear what was being said downstairs.

"Police business, at this time of night?" Professor Balboni's voice boomed out. "What is this all about?"

"I apologize for the late hour, Professor Balboni. But I wanted to warn you about certain developments." It was a man's voice, low but urgent.

"I have no idea what you're talking about," said Balboni.

"I understand why you might not trust me. But tonight it's vital that you take me into your confidence."

The voices faded as the two men moved into the dining room.

"What will happen to you if the police find me here?" whispered Lorenzo.

"Don't worry," Laura answered. "Papa can talk

his way out of this. He always does." She touched her fingers to his lips. "Stay here. Don't make a sound."

"Where are you going?"

"To help distract our visitor." She shot him a tense smile. "Papa says I'm clever at that. Let's find out how clever."

Through the closed bedroom door, he heard her footsteps creak down the stairs to join the two men in the dining room.

"How naughty of you, Papa! Didn't you offer our visitor any refreshments?" came her cheerful voice. "Signore, I'm Laura, Professor Balboni's daughter. Can I pour you a glass of wine? Perhaps you'd like cake and coffee? Alda, why don't you bring us a tray? I don't want our visitor to think we've forgotten how to be proper hosts."

Though he could not hear the man's responses, Lorenzo heard Laura's laughter, the bright clatter of chinaware and Alda's footsteps moving back and forth between dining room and kitchen. With her entrance, Laura had managed to transform a stranger's alarming intrusion into an evening of cake and conversation. Not even a policeman could resist her charm. Now the visitor was laughing as well, and Lorenzo heard the pop of a wine bottle being uncorked.

Neck aching from crouching too long at the door, he straightened and massaged away the soreness. For the first time he looked around and realized he was in Laura's room. It smelled like her, bright and floral, lavender and sunshine. There was a cheerful disorder to the space, her books stacked haphazardly on the bedside table, a sweater tossed over a chair, a vanity table cluttered with creams and powders and brushes. He touched a brush, its bristles tangled with blond strands. He imagined stroking that brush through her hair, like sifting through gold.

The bookshelves were filled with charming Laura clutter. A collection of porcelain pigs, arranged in a group as though in porcine conversation. A ground-down cake of cello rosin. A bowl with tennis balls. And more books; how Laura loved her books! He saw volumes of poetry, a biography of Mozart, a collection of plays by Ibsen. And a whole shelf of love stories, something he had not expected. His fierce, no-nonsense Laura was a reader of romance novels? There was so much he did not know about her, so much he would never know, because tomorrow night, he would be fleeing Venice.

The thought of never seeing her again made him press his hand to his heart, the pain as real as a blow to the chest. To be standing here in her room, breathing in her scent, only made the anguish worse.

From downstairs came the sound of her voice, sweetly calling out: "Good night, signore! Please don't keep Papa up too late!" Then up the stairs she came, humming a tune as she climbed, as though she hadn't a care in the world.

She stepped into the bedroom, closed the door behind her, and leaned back against it, her face brittle with tension. At his questioning look, she gave a sharp shake of the head.

"He's not leaving," she whispered.

"What's your father going to do?"

"Get him drunk. Keep him talking."

"Why is he here?"

"I don't know. That's what frightens me. He seems to know far too much about us. He claims he wants to help, if only Papa will cooperate." She turned off the light, and with the room now dark, she dared to open the curtain. Peering out the window she said, "I don't see anyone in the street, but they still might be watching the house." She turned to him. "You can't leave now. It's not safe out there."

"I need to go home. I need to warn my family."

"There's nothing you can do for them, Lorenzo. Not tonight." She paused as the sound of men's laughter rumbled up from the dining room. "Papa knows how to handle this. Yes, he's good at it." She seemed to take courage from that certainty. "He can charm anyone."

So can you. In the darkness, all he could see was her silhouette, framed by the window. There were so many things he wanted to say to her, so many secrets he wanted to confess, but despair swallowed up his words.

"You have to stay here. Really, would that be so terrible?" she asked with a soft laugh. "To be trapped with me tonight?" She turned to look at him, and as their gazes met in the darkness, she went still.

He grasped her hand and pressed it to his lips. "Laura," he whispered. That was all he said, just her name. With that one word, spoken so tenderly, he revealed all his secrets.

And she heard them. As she stepped toward him, his arms were already open to welcome her. The taste of her lips was as intoxicating as wine, and he could not have enough of her, could never have enough. They both knew that heartache would surely come of this, but the flames had already leapt beyond their control, fed by five years of separation and longing.

Breathless, they both came up for air and stared at each other in the darkness. Moonlight shone in through the gap in the curtain, illuminating one glorious sliver of Laura's face.

"How I missed you," she whispered. "I wrote so many letters, telling you what I felt."

"I never got them."

"Because I tore them up. I couldn't bear the thought that you didn't feel the same way."

"I did." He framed her face in his hands. "Oh Laura, I did."

"Why did you never tell me?"

"After everything that happened, I couldn't imagine that we'd ever be . . ."

"Ever be together?"

He sighed and his hands dropped to his sides. "Tonight, it seems more impossible than ever."

"Lorenzo," she whispered and pressed her lips to his, not a kiss of desire but reassurance. "It will never happen if we don't imagine it first. So that's what we must do."

"I want you to be happy. That's all I've ever wanted."

"And that's why you stayed away from me."

"I have nothing to offer. What can I promise you?"

"Things will change! The world may be insane now, but it won't stay that way. There are too many good people. We'll make it all right again."

"Is that what your father tells you?"

"It's what I believe. It's what I *have* to believe, or there's nothing left to hope for, and I can't live without hope."

Now he smiled, too. "My ferocious Laura. Did you know I was once afraid of you?"

"Yes." She laughed. "Papa says I must learn not to be so frightening."

"But that's why I love you."

"And do you know why I love you?"

He shook his head. "I can't imagine."

"Because *you're* fierce, too. About your music, about your family. About things that matter. At Ca' Foscari, I met so many boys who told me they want to be rich or famous, or they want a holiday house in the country. But those are just things to *want*, not things to *care* about."

"And were you ever tempted by one of those boys? Even a little?"

"How could I be? I could only think about you, standing onstage that night. How confident you were, how commanding. When you played, I could hear your soul singing to mine." She pressed her forehead against his. "I've never felt that with anyone else. Only you."

"I don't know when I'll return. I can't ask you to wait."

"Remember what I said? It will never happen if

we don't imagine it first. So that's what we must do: picture ourselves together someday in the future. I think you'll look quite distinguished when you're older! You'll have silver hair, here and here." She touched his temples. "When you smile, you'll have handsome creases around your eyes. You'll wear funny spectacles, just like Papa does."

"And you'll be just as beautiful as you are tonight."

She laughed. "Oh no, I'll be fat from all our babies!"

"But every bit as beautiful."

"You see? That's how it could be for us. Growing old together. We mustn't stop believing it, because someday . . ."

The shriek of air raid sirens suddenly pierced the night.

They both turned to the window and Laura pushed open the curtains. On the street below, neighbors were gathering to scan the sky for aircraft. Despite frequent air raid sirens, the city had never known an aerial attack, and Venetians had grown cavalier about the wails that regularly interrupted their sleep. Even if bombs were to fall, where, in this city built on water, were they expected to take shelter?

Laura called down from her darkened window: "Signore, is this just another drill?"

"With all these clouds and mist, it's certainly not a night for an air raid!" the man yelled back. "A pilot wouldn't be able to see ten feet in front of him."

"Why are the sirens on?"

"Who knows?" He called out to a trio of men who stood stomping in the cold, their cigarettes glowing. "Have you heard any news?"

"Nothing on the radio. My wife is calling her sister in Mestre to see if she's seen anything."

Up and down the street more and more people emerged, bundled in coats and shawls, shouting questions over the unceasing racket. Instead of fear, what Lorenzo heard in their voices was puzzlement and excitement, and even a note of festivity, as if this were a party in the street to the tune of sirens.

The bedroom door suddenly creaked open and Professor Balboni slipped into the room. "Our visitor's gone at last," he whispered.

"Papa, what did he say? Why was he here?" asked Laura.

"Dear God, if what he said was true—the things he told me—"

"What things?"

"The SS will soon be going door-to-door, making arrests." He looked at Lorenzo. "There's no time left. You must disappear *tonight*. With these sirens going, with all the chaos in the streets, you might be able to slip away."

"I need to go home. I need to tell them," said Lorenzo, turning to the door.

Balboni caught him by the arm. "It's too late to save them. Your family is on the list. They may already be headed to your house."

"My sister is only fourteen years old! I can't leave her behind!" Lorenzo pulled free and ran out of the room.

"Lorenzo, wait!" called Laura as she followed

him down the stairs. At the front door, she grabbed his arm, pulled him to a halt. "Please listen to Papa!"

"I have to warn them. You know I do."

"Papa, talk to him," Laura pleaded as her father came down the stairs. "Tell him it's too dangerous."

Balboni gave a sad shake of the head. "I think he's made his choice, and we can't change his mind." He looked at Lorenzo. "Keep to the shadows, boy. If you're able to get your family out of Cannaregio, make for the monastery in Padua. They'll give you sanctuary, until someone can take you to the border." He grasped Lorenzo's shoulders. "When this is all over, when Italy comes back to its senses, we'll see you here again. And we'll celebrate."

Lorenzo turned to Laura. She had her hand pressed to her mouth, trying to hold back tears. He pulled her against him and felt her body shuddering with the effort not to cry. "Never stop believing in us," he whispered.

"I won't. Not ever."

"Then it will happen." He pressed his lips to hers and drank in one last taste of her. "We will *make* it happen."

13

Out into the night he went, his scarf wrapped around his face to ward off any unwelcome stares. The air raid sirens continued their unceasing wails, as if the sky itself were shrieking in despair. Drawn out of their homes on this strange night, a small crowd had gathered in the Campo della Carità, hungry for news and trading rumors. Had this been a real air raid, Death would have found them out in the open, doomed by their own curiosity. But like every other night before it, no bombs fell on Venice, and those who lingered too long outside suffered only from cold hands and feet, and in the morning, from bleary-eyed regret that they had gone to bed so late.

No one saw the young man who slipped past them in the shadows.

On this night of mist and chaos, Lorenzo made his way unnoticed across the bridge and through the neighborhood of San Polo. His greatest challenge lay ahead: how to move his family out of the city before daybreak. Could Mama make it all the way to Padua on foot? Should they send Marco and Pia ahead? If the family split up, how and where would they reunite?

He heard screams and the sound of shattering glass, and he darted for the shadows. Peering around the corner, he watched as a man and woman were dragged out of a house and forced to their knees in the street. Broken shards of glass rained from an upstairs window, followed by books and papers that tumbled down like wounded birds, to land in an ever-growing pile on the street. The kneeling woman sobbed and pleaded, but the air raid sirens drowned out her cries.

A match flame flickered to life in the darkness. Tossed onto the mound of papers, the flame quickly bloomed into an inferno.

Lorenzo backed away from the brightening firelight and darted down a different street to circle north, through Santa Croce. As he crossed the bridge into Cannaregio, he spied the hellish glow of another fire ahead. *My street. My house.*

He sprinted around the corner to Calle del Forno and stared in horror at the bonfire roaring in the street, devouring a mound of books. Grandpapa's books. Scattered across the cobblestones was a sea of broken glass, the shards reflecting the firelight like small pools of flame.

The door to his home was splintered wide open. He did not need to step inside to see the destruction within: the shattered crockery, the ripped curtains.

"They're gone, Lorenzo!" a girl's voice called out.

He spun around and saw his twelve-year-old neighbor Isabella watching him forlornly from across the street. "The police took them away. Then the Blackshirts came and set fire to everything. They were like crazy people. Why did they have to break the dishes? Papa told me to stay inside, but I saw it from my window. I saw the whole thing."

"Where are they? Where is my family?"

"They're at Marco Foscarini. Everyone is there."

"Why were they taken to the school?"

"The policeman said they're going to be sent to a work camp. He told Papa not to worry about them, because it will just be for a little while. When everything calms down, they'll come back again. He said it will be like a holiday away from home. Papa says there's nothing we can do about it. It's just the way it has to be."

Lorenzo looked down at the blackened ashes, all that remained of his grandfather Alberto's prized library of music. In the shadowy periphery, a lone volume had survived the flames. He reached down to retrieve it, and the stench of smoke rose from the singed pages. It was Alberto's collection of Gypsy melodies, tunes that Lorenzo had known since the cradle. The same tunes Pia hummed late at night when she combed her hair. He stood cradling the precious music book, worried about his sister, thinking how terrified she must be. He thought about his mother, with her aching knees and weak lungs. How would she survive hard labor in a work camp?

"Are you going with them, Lorenzo?" Isabella

asked. "If you hurry, you can catch up and you'll be together. It won't be so bad at the camp. That's what the policeman said."

He looked up at the ruined windows of his home. If he left now, he could be well on his way to Padua by sunrise. From there he'd have to head northwest into the mountains, and across the Swiss border. It's what Professor Balboni had urged him to do: Run. Forget his family and save himself.

And when the war is over, he thought, *how can I face them again, knowing that I abandoned them to the miseries of a labor camp?* He imagined the look of betrayal in Pia's eyes. That's all he could think of: the look in his sister's eyes.

"Lorenzo?"

"Thank you, Bella." Gently he placed a hand on the girl's head. "Stay well. Someday we'll meet again."

"Are you running away?"

"No." He tucked the music book under his coat. "I'm going to find my family."

It was Pia who spotted him. Over the din of wailing children and babies, he heard her shout his name and saw her arms frantically waving for his attention. So many people were crowded into the makeshift detention center at Collegio Marco Foscarini that he had to push past stunned old men rocking in despair, had to step over families who had simply collapsed on the floor in weary heaps.

Pia launched herself so joyously into his arms that he stumbled back from the force of her embrace. "I thought we'd never see you again! Marco said you ran away, but I knew you wouldn't do that. I knew you wouldn't leave us!"

His mother and father crowded in to embrace him as well, wrapping him in a smothering tangle of arms. Only when they finally released him did his brother, Marco, come forward to give him a firm clap on the back.

"We had no idea where you went," said Marco.

"I was at the Balbonis' house when I heard the air raid sirens."

"It was all a ruse," Marco said bitterly. "They used the sirens to take us by surprise. No one could hear what was going on. And we still have no news of Grandpapa. There are rumors that they even raided his nursing home." Marco glanced at their mother, who had sunk onto a bench, clutching her coat tighter. He said softly: "They pulled her straight out of bed. Didn't even let her get properly dressed. We grabbed what we could before they dragged us onto the street."

"I saw the house," said Lorenzo. "The Black-shirts broke every window, burned every book. It's happening all over the city."

"And you had a chance to escape? Why the hell didn't you run? You could be on your way to the border!"

"What about Pia? Mama? We're a family, Marco. We have to stay together."

"How long do you think you'll last in a labor camp? How long do you think *they'll* last?"

"Quiet. You'll scare Pia."

"I'm *not* scared," said Pia. "Not now that we're

all together." She took Lorenzo's hand. "Come, look at what I did. You'll be so pleased."

"What?"

"When I heard them banging on the door, I ran straight to your room. I kept it under my coat, so they wouldn't see it." She pulled him over to the bench where their mother was sitting and reached underneath.

He looked down at what Pia was holding and for a moment he couldn't speak, he was so moved by what his sister had done for him. Inside the violin case, La Dianora was still snug and safe in her velvet cradle. He touched the varnished wood, and even in that chilly room, it felt warm to his fingertips, as alive as flesh.

Through tears, he looked at his sister. "Thank you." He wrapped his arms around her. "Thank you, darling Pia."

"I knew you'd come back for it. I knew you'd come back for *us*."

"And here I am." Right where he needed to be.

He woke up the next morning to the sound of crying children.

Stiff from sleeping on the floor, Lorenzo groaned as he sat up and rubbed his eyes. The light that shone in through the assembly hall's filthy windows tinted every face in the room a cold, drab gray. Nearby, an exhausted woman was trying to hush her fretting infant. An old man rocked back and forth, babbling words that only he could understand. Everywhere Lorenzo looked, he saw slumped shoulders and stunned faces, many of whom he recognized. There were the Perlmutters, who had the daughter with the cleft lip, and the Sanguinettis, whose fourteen-year-old son had once been Lorenzo's violin student, until the boy's singular lack of interest put an end to the lessons. There were the Polaccos, who owned the tailor shop, and Mr. Berger, who was once bank president, and old Mrs. Ravenna, who always seemed to argue with Mama whenever they met in the square. Whether young or old, scholars or laborers, they had all been reduced to this same state of misery.

"When will they bring us food?" Mrs. Perlmutter wailed. "My children are hungry!"

"We're all hungry," a man retorted.

"You can go without food. The children can't."

"Speak for yourself."

"That's all you can think about, is it? Yourself and no one else?"

Mr. Perlmutter placed a calming hand on his wife's arm. "This doesn't help anyone. Please, let it go." He smiled at their children. "Don't you worry. They'll bring us something to eat soon."

"When, Papa?"

"By lunchtime, I'm certain of it. You'll see."

But lunchtime came and went, and so did dinnertime. No food appeared that day, or the next. They had only water to drink from the bathroom tap.

At night, the hungry wails of the children kept Lorenzo awake.

Curled up on the floor next to Pia and Marco, he closed his eyes and tried not to think about food,

but how could he not? He remembered the meals
he'd enjoyed at Professor Balboni's table: the clear-
est, brightest consommés he'd ever tasted. Crisp
fish from the lagoon, so tiny that he had eaten them
bones and all. He thought of cakes and wines and
the heady smells of a roasting chicken.

His sister moaned in her sleep, pursued by hunger into her dreams.

He wrapped his arm around her and whispered:
"Hush, Pia, I'm here. Everything will be fine." She
curled up against him and settled back to sleep, but
he could not.

He was wide awake when the first sack came
tumbling through the open window.

It nearly landed on the head of a sleeping woman.
She startled awake and cried out in the darkness:
"Now they're trying to kill us! Trying to crush our
heads while we sleep!"

A second sack dropped into the room and something rolled out, rumbling across the floor.

"Who's throwing things at us? Why are they
doing this?"

Lorenzo climbed onto the bench and peered out
of the high window. He saw two shadowy figures
crouched below, one of them about to swing yet a
third sack up and over the high sill into the room.

"Hey, you!" Lorenzo called out. "What are you
doing?"

One of the figures looked up. The moon was full
and under its stark illumination, he saw the face of
an elderly woman dressed all in black. She placed a
finger to her lips in a plea for silence, then she and

her companion scurried from the building and slipped away into the darkness.

"Apples!" a woman called out in delight. "There are apples here!"

Someone lit a candle, and by its meager glow they saw the bounty that had spilled from the sacks. Loaves of bread. Wedges of cheese wrapped in newspapers. A cloth bag of boiled potatoes.

"First feed the children!" a woman pleaded. "The children!"

But people were already scooping up the food, desperate for some small scrap before it all vanished. Apples disappeared into pockets. Two women clawed at each other, fighting for a packet of cheese. A man crammed a potato into his mouth, greedily devouring it before anyone could snatch it from him.

Marco dove into the melee and emerged a moment later clutching half a loaf of bread, all he could salvage for their family. They huddled together guarding their treasure as Marco tore the bread into five pieces and handed a portion to each. It was tough as leather, at least a day old, but to Lorenzo it was as welcome as the tenderest of cakes. He savored each bite, eyes closed in pleasure as he let the morsels dissolve into yeasty sweetness on his tongue. He thought of all the other bread he'd eaten in his life and how thoughtlessly he'd chewed it without really tasting, because bread was like air, something you took for granted, the unsung staple at every meal.

As he licked the last crumbs from his fingers, he noticed that his father had not touched his own portion, but was merely staring down at the bread in his hands.

"Papa, eat," Lorenzo said.

"I'm not hungry."

"How can you not be hungry? You haven't eaten in two days!"

"I don't want it." His father held out the bread to Lorenzo. "Here. It's for you and Pia and Marco."

"Don't be crazy, Papa," said Marco. "You need to eat."

Bruno shook his head. "This is my fault, it's all my fault. I should have listened to you, Marco, and to Professor Balboni. We should have left Italy months ago. Stubborn old fool, that's what I am!" The bread fell to the floor and he dropped his face in his hands. He rocked forward, body shuddering with sobs. Never before had Lorenzo seen him cry. Could this broken man really be his father, who always insisted he knew what was best for the family? Who stubbornly kept the luthier shop open for business six days a week, even as the clientele dwindled away? What fortitude it must have taken for Bruno to hide his doubts these five years, to bear the full burden of every decision, good or bad. And this is where his choices had led them. Lorenzo was so shocked by the sight of his father crumbling that he didn't know what to say or do.

But Mama did. She wrapped her generous arms around her husband and pulled his face against her shoulder. "No, no, Bruno, this is not your fault," she murmured. "I couldn't abandon Papa. I didn't want to leave, either, so it's my fault, too. We made the choice together."

"And now we suffer together."

"It won't be forever. And really, how terrible could it be in the camp? I'm not afraid to work, and I know you aren't. You have always worked so hard. What's important is that we're together, isn't that right?" She stroked back the thinning wisps of his hair and kissed the top of his head. "Isn't it?"

Lorenzo could not remember the last time he'd seen his parents kiss or embrace. At home they always seemed like separate planets moving in their own orbits, circling close but never touching. He could not imagine them ever burning for each other, the way he burned for Laura, but here they were, clinging like lovers. Did he ever really know his parents?

"Papa, please eat," Pia begged, and she placed the chunk of bread in Bruno's hand.

Bruno stared at it, as if he'd never seen bread before and did not know what to do with it. When he did begin to eat, it was without apparent pleasure, as if consuming it was a duty, and he did it only to please his family.

"There, now." His wife smiled. "Everything will be fine."

"Yes." Bruno took a deep breath and sat up straight, the family patriarch back in control. "Everything will be fine."

At dawn on the third day, the doors burst open.

Lorenzo lurched awake to the sound of boots thudding across the floor. He scrambled to his feet as uniformed men fanned into the room. They wore the insignia of the fascist Guardia Nazionale Repubblicana.

Over the screams of terrified children, a voice boomed out: "Attention! *Silence!*" The officer did not step over the threshold but addressed them from the doorway, as if the air in the room was foul and he had no wish to pollute his lungs.

Pia slipped her hand into Lorenzo's. She was shaking.

"Article Seven of the Carta di Verona has classified you as enemy aliens," the officer announced. "Under police order number five, issued December first, you will be transported to an internment camp. The ministry has generously exempted those who are gravely ill or elderly, but you have all been deemed able-bodied and eligible for transport."

"Then Grandpapa is safe?" Pia said. "They won't take him from the nursing home?"

"Shhh." Lorenzo gave her hand a warning squeeze. *Don't draw their attention.*

"The train is waiting for you," said the officer. "After you board, you are each allowed to write one letter. I suggest you tell your friends and neighbors that you are well, and they should not be concerned. I assure you, your letters will be delivered. Now it's time to gather your belongings. Bring only what you can carry to the station."

"You see?" Eloisa whispered to Bruno. "They're even allowing us to send letters. And Papa can stay in his nursing home. I will write to him, so he won't worry about us. And you must write to Professor Balboni. Tell him that he frightened us for nothing and everything is fine."

With so many families, so many young children among them, their procession to the train station was a slow one. They moved in a shuffling line past familiar shopwindows and over the same foot-bridge that Lorenzo had crossed countless times before. Bystanders gathered to watch in eerie silence, as if viewing a parade of ghosts. Among the faces of the spectators, he spotted the neighbor girl Isabella. She raised her arm to wave to him, but her father grabbed her wrist and yanked it down. As Lorenzo passed, the man would not look him in the eye, but stared down at the cobblestones, as if merely meeting his gaze would doom him as well.

The silent parade crossed the piazza, where, on any other day, they would hear laughter and chatter, women calling out to their children. But today there was only the sound of shuffling feet, so many feet, moving in a weary column. Those who witnessed the passing did not dare to speak out in protest.

In that silence, the lone voice that suddenly called out was all the more startling.

"Lorenzo, here! I am here!"

At first all he saw was the glint of sunlight on blond hair, and the parting of the crowd as she pushed forward, pleading: "Let me through! I need to get through!"

Then all at once there she was, her arms flung around him, her lips on his. She tasted of salt and tears.

"I love you," said Lorenzo. "Wait for me."

"I promise. And you must promise to come back to me."

"You, girl!" a guard barked. "Move away!"

Laura was wrenched from Lorenzo's arms, and he stumbled back into the moving herd, which carried him forward, ever forward.

"Promise me!" he heard her call out.

He turned, desperate for one last glimpse of her, but her face was already lost in the crowd. All he saw was one pale hand raised in farewell.

"They're blind, all of them," said Marco. "They cover their eyes and refuse to see what's happening."

As their parents and sister dozed beside them, lulled to sleep by the hypnotic clacks of the train, the brothers spoke softly to each other.

"Those letters home, they mean nothing. They let us write them to keep us calm. To distract us." He looked at Lorenzo. "You wrote to Laura, didn't you?"

"Are you saying my letter won't be delivered?"

"Oh, she'll probably get it. But why, do you think?"

"I don't know what you're really asking."

Marco snorted. "Because you're as blind as everyone else, little brother! You float through life on a cloud, dreaming only of your music, believing that oh yes, all will turn out for the best! You'll marry Laura Balboni and have perfect children and spend your lives happily ever after, playing beautiful music."

"At least I won't be bitter and angry, like you."

"You know why I'm bitter? Because I see the

truth. Your letter will be delivered. So will Pia's and Mama's." He glanced at their sleeping parents, who had curled up against each other, arms entwined. "Did you see the nonsense Mama wrote? *Our train has comfortable third-class seats. They promise that our accommodations at the camp will be equally acceptable.* As if we're headed to some resort on Como! Our friends and neighbors will believe that all's well, that we're sitting like tourists on the train, so they won't worry. Just like Papa refuses to worry. All his life he's worked with his hands and he won't believe what he can't see and touch. He lacks the imagination to consider the worst. And that's why nobody ever fights back, because we all want to believe the best. Because it's too frightening to imagine the possibilities." He looked at Lorenzo. "Have you noticed which direction this train is taking us?"

"How can I tell? They've kept all the window shades down."

"Because they don't want us to see where we're going. But even through the shades, you can see on which side the sun is shining."

"They told us we're going to the internment camp in Fossoli. That's where they send everyone."

"That's what they say. But look at the light, Lorenzo. See which side of the train it's shining on? We're not headed to Fossoli." Grimly, Marco stared straight ahead and said, softly: "This train is going north."

Julia ✑

14

Rob is furious with me. I hear it in the slam of the front door and his agitated footsteps as he storms into the kitchen.

"Why did you cancel your appointment with Dr. Rose?" he demands.

I don't turn to look at him, but continue chopping carrots and potatoes for dinner. Roast chicken is on the menu tonight, rubbed with olive oil and lemon, seasoned with rosemary and sea salt. It will be a meal just for the two of us because Lily is still staying with Val. It is far too quiet with her gone, and the house does not feel right. It feels as if I've slipped into some sad parallel universe, and the real house with the real me exists somewhere else. A house where we are all happy again, where my daughter loves me and my husband is not standing in the kitchen, glaring.

"I wasn't in the mood to see her," I tell him.

"Not in the *mood*? Do you know how hard it

was for her to fit you into her schedule on such short notice?"

"The psychiatrist was your idea, not mine."

He gives a frustrated laugh. "Yeah, she predicted you'd be resistant. She said denial is part of your problem."

Calmly I set down the knife and turn to face this parallel-universe version of Rob. Unlike my calm, starched-shirt husband, the man I see now is flushed and agitated and his tie hangs askew. "You've been to see her? You two are already discussing me?"

"Of course we are! I'm at wit's end. I needed to talk to *someone*."

"And what did you tell her?"

"That you're so obsessed with that damn piece of music, you won't address the real problem. That you've withdrawn from Lily. And you've withdrawn from me."

"If someone stabbed *you* in the leg, you'd withdraw, too."

"I know you think Lily's the problem, but Dr. Rose spent three hours observing her. She saw a perfectly normal and charming three-year-old. There was no violent behavior, no sign of pathology whatsoever."

I stare at him, stunned by what I've just heard. "You brought my daughter to see a psychiatrist, and you didn't bother to tell me?"

"You think this has been easy for Lily? She spends more time at Val's than she does here and she's confused. Meanwhile, you're calling Rome every day. I saw the phone bills. That poor shopkeeper probably wonders why the crazy lady won't leave him alone!"

The word *crazy* hits me like a slap. It's the first time he's said it to my face, but I know he's been thinking it all along. I'm his crazy wife, the daughter of another crazy woman.

"Oh God, Julia. I'm sorry." He sighs and says, quietly: "Please. Go see Dr. Rose."

"What difference would it make? It sounds like you two have already diagnosed me in absentia."

"She's a good psychiatrist. She's easy to talk to, and I think she really cares about her patients. Lily liked her right away. I think you will, too."

I turn back to the cutting board and pick up the knife. Begin slicing carrots again, slowly and deliberately. Even as he comes up behind me and wraps his arms around my waist, I continue slicing, my blade thudding against wood.

"I'm doing this for us," he whispers and kisses the back of my neck. The heat of his breath makes me shudder, as if a stranger is groping me. Not the husband I adored, not the man I've loved for more than a decade. "It's because I love you both. You and Lily. My two best girls in the world."

After Rob falls asleep that night, I climb out of bed and creep downstairs to his computer, where I search online for Dr. Diana Rose. Rob is right; I have been so obsessed with hunting down the origins of *Incendio* that I haven't paid attention to what is going on in my own home. I need to know more about this woman who has already diagnosed me as *resistant* and *in denial*. She has skillfully worked her way into my family, charming my daughter, impressing my husband, yet I know nothing about her.

Google turns up dozens of hits for "Dr. Diana Rose, Boston." Her professional website lists her specialty (psychiatry), practice information (downtown Boston address, multiple hospital affiliations), and education (Boston University and Harvard Medical School). But it's the photo that rivets my attention.

While Rob was singing her praises, he neglected to tell me that Dr. Rose is a stunningly beautiful brunette.

I click on the next Google link. It's a news item from Worcester, Massachusetts, about a court case where Dr. Rose was the expert witness. She testified that Mrs. Lisa Verdon was a danger to her own children. Because of that testimony, the court awarded custody to their father.

Fear ties a knot in my stomach.

I click on the next link. It's a different court case, and I see the words *competency hearing*. Dr. Rose, testifying for the state of Massachusetts, recommended involuntary commitment of a Mr. Lester Heist because he was a danger to himself.

In the next dozen Web pages I visit, I spot that word again and again. *Competency*. This is Dr. Rose's expertise. She determines if patients are a danger to themselves or others. If they should be shut away in institutions the way my mother was.

I exit Google and stare at the computer screen, where I notice a new photo is displayed as wallpaper. When did Rob change it? Only a week ago, there was an image of all three of us, posing in our back garden. Now there is a photo of only Lily, her hair a bright halo in the sunshine. I feel as if I've been erased from our family, and if I look down, I'll find my arms are fading to invisibility. How long before there's a different woman's face on this screen? A doe-eyed brunette who thinks my daughter is sweet and charming and perfectly normal?

Dr. Diana Rose is as attractive in person as she is in her Web page photograph. Her fifth-floor office has large windows that overlook the Charles River, but the view is obscured by sheer window shades. Those covered windows make me feel claustrophobic, as if I'm shut away in a white box with white furniture, and if I don't say the right things, if I can't prove I'm sane, this woman will have me sealed in here forever.

Her first questions are innocuous enough. Where was I born, where did I grow up, how is my general state of health? She has green eyes and flawless skin and her eggshell silk blouse is just sheer enough to reveal the outline of her bra. I wonder if my husband noticed those same details at his sessions on this same couch where I'm sitting. Her voice is soothing as honey, and she's good at making it seem that she really cares about my well-being, but I think she's a thief. She's stolen my daughter's affection and my husband's loyalty. When I tell her I'm a professional musician with a degree from New England Conservatory, I think I see her lip curl up in disdain. Does she think musicians aren't true professionals? Her diplomas and certificates and awards are framed and displayed all over her wall, documentary proof that she's superior to any mere musician.

"So you think it all started when you played that piece of music, *Incendio*," she says. "Tell me more about the music. You said you found it in Rome."

"In an antiques store," I say.

"What made you buy it?"

"I collect music. I'm always on the hunt for something I've never heard before. Something unique and beautiful."

"And you knew this piece would sound beautiful, just by looking at it?"

"Yes. When I read music, I can hear the notes in my head. I thought it might work as an arrangement for my quartet. When I got home, I played it on my violin. That's when Lily . . ." I stop. "That's when she changed."

"And you're convinced *Incendio* caused this."

"There's something very wrong about this piece. Something dark and disturbing. It has a negative energy, and I felt it the first time I played it. I think Lily felt it, too. I think she reacted to it."

"And that's why she hurt you." Dr. Rose's expression is perfectly neutral, but she can't disguise the skepticism in her voice. It's as obvious to me as a single sour note in an otherwise perfect performance. "Because of the music's negative energy."

"I don't know what else to call it. There's just something *wrong* about it."

She nods as if she understands, but of course she

doesn't. "Is this why you've been making all those phone calls to Rome?"

"I want to know where this music comes from and what its history is. It might explain why it has this effect on Lily. I've been trying to reach the man who sold me the music, but he doesn't answer the phone. His granddaughter wrote me a letter a few weeks ago, saying she'd ask him to find out more information. But I've heard nothing since then."

Dr. Rose takes a breath, rearranges her position. A nonverbal cue that she's about to shift strategy. "How do you feel about your daughter, Mrs. Ansdell?" she asks quietly.

That makes me pause, because I am not sure of my answer. I remember Lily smiling up at me when she was a newborn, and how I thought at the time: *This will always be the happiest moment of my life.* I remember the night she burned with a fever, how frantic I was that I might lose her. Then I think of the day I looked down to see that shard of glass embedded in my leg, and heard my daughter chanting *hurt Mommy, hurt Mommy.*

"Mrs. Ansdell?"

"I love her, of course," I answer automatically.

"Even though she attacked you?"

"Yes."

"Even though she doesn't seem like the same child."

"Yes."

"Do you ever feel the urge to hurt her in return?"

I stare at her. "What?"

"Feelings like that aren't unusual," she says, sounding quite reasonable. "Even the most patient mother can be pushed to the edge and spank or slap a child."

"I've *never* hurt her. I've never wanted to hurt her!"

"Have you ever felt the urge to hurt yourself?" Oh, how easily she slipped that in. I can see in which direction her questions are taking us.

"Why are you asking that?" I say.

"You've been injured twice. You were stabbed in the leg. You fell down the stairs."

"I didn't stab myself. Or throw myself down the stairs."

She sighs, as if I'm too dense to understand what's obvious to everyone else. "Mrs. Ansdell, no one else was there to see those incidents. Is it possible they didn't occur quite the way you remember?"

"They happened *exactly* the way I described them."

"I'm only trying to assess the situation. There's no reason to be hostile."

Is that what she hears in my voice? I take a deep breath to calm down, even though I have every reason to be hostile. My marriage is collapsing, my daughter wants to hurt me, and there sits Dr. Rose, so serene and in control. I wonder if her life is as perfect as she appears to be. Maybe she's a secret drunk or a shoplifter or a nymphomaniac.

Maybe she steals other women's husbands.

"Look, I don't know why I'm talking to you," I say. "I think this is a huge waste of your time as well as mine."

"Your husband's concerned about you. That's

why you're here. He said you've lost weight and you're not sleeping well."

"What else has he told you?"

"That you've become alienated from your daughter, and from him as well. That you seem so preoccupied, you don't seem to hear what he says. Which is why I need to ask you this. Are you hearing other voices?"

"What do you mean?"

"Voices talking in your head? People who aren't there, telling you to do things? Maybe hurt yourself?"

"You're asking if I'm psychotic." I burst out laughing. "The answer, Dr. Rose, isn't just *no*. It's *hell no!*"

"I hope you understand that it's just something I have to ask. Your husband's worried about your daughter's welfare, and since he has to work during the day, we need to be sure she's safe alone with you at home."

At last we've come to the real reason I'm sitting in a psychiatrist's office. They think I'm a danger to Lily. That I'm a baby-killing monster like my mother was, and Lily must be protected from me.

"I'm told your daughter's now staying with your aunt. That isn't a long-term solution," says Dr. Rose. "Your husband wants his daughter to come home eventually, but he also wants to be sure it's safe for her to do so."

"Don't you think I want her home, too? Since the day she was born, I've hardly been apart from her. With her gone, I feel like part of me's missing."

"Even if you do want her home, think about

what's happened. You were hours late picking her up from day care and you didn't even realize it. You believe your daughter is violent and wants to harm you. You are obsessed with a piece of music that you think is evil." She pauses. "And you have a history in your family of psychosis."

It all paints an undeniably ugly picture. Anyone who hears the relentless litany of facts could not argue with her conclusions. So what she says next comes as no surprise.

"Before I can feel comfortable about your daughter returning home, I believe you need further evaluation. I recommend a period of observation in an inpatient setting. There's a very good clinic outside Worcester, which I'm sure you'll find comfortable. This will be completely voluntary on your part. Think of it as a short vacation. A chance to shed all responsibility for a while and just focus on yourself."

"How short a vacation are we talking about?"

"I can't be specific at this point."

"So it could be weeks. Even months."

"It depends on how much progress you make."

"And who'd be the one to determine my progress? You?" My retort makes her lean back in her chair. *Patient extremely hostile* will certainly be in her notes. It's yet another detail that will reinforce the disturbing picture of Julia Ansdell, crazy mom.

"Let me emphasize, this period of evaluation is completely voluntary," she says. "You can sign out of the clinic anytime you want to."

She makes it sound as if I actually have a choice, as if what happens next is entirely my decision, but we both know I'm boxed in. If I say no, I'll lose my daughter and most likely my husband. In truth, I've already lost them both. All I have left now is my freedom, and even that is entirely up to Dr. Rose. She only needs to declare me a danger to myself or others, and the asylum door will slam shut.

I feel her eyes on me as I consider my response. *Must stay calm, must stay agreeable.* "I'll need some time to get ready for this," I say. "I want to talk to my husband first. And I need to make sure Aunt Val is able to help with Lily."

"Of course. I understand."

"Since I might be gone for a while, there are practical details to arrange."

"We aren't talking about forever, Mrs. Ansdell."

But for my mother, it *was* forever. For my mother, a mental institution was the final stop in her short, turbulent life.

Dr. Rose walks me out to the waiting room, where Rob has been sitting. To be certain I made it to this appointment, he drove me here himself, and I see the questioning look he gives Dr. Rose. She nods to him, her silent assurance that all went well and the crazy wife will cooperate with their plans.

And I do cooperate. What alternative do I have? I sit meekly in the car while Rob drives. When we get home, he lingers for a while, watching to make sure I don't jump out a window or slit my wrists. I putter around the kitchen, set a kettle on the stove, trying to appear as normal as I can, even though my nerves are so frayed they could snap at any instant. When at last he leaves to go back to work,

I'm so relieved I let out a sob and collapse into a chair at the kitchen table.

So this is what it's like to go insane.

I drop my head in my hands and think about mental hospitals. *A clinic* was what Dr. Rose called it, but I know what kind of place they want to send me to. I've seen a photo of the institution where my mother died. It had beautiful trees and sweeping lawns; it also had locks on the windows. Is that the sort of place where I too will end my days?

The kettle screams for my attention.

I get up to pour hot water into the teapot. Then I sit down to confront the stack of mail that's accumulated on the kitchen table. There's three days' worth, still unopened; that's how distracted we've been, too embroiled in our family crisis to deal with the day-to-day issues like ironing shirts or paying bills. No wonder Rob looks so rumpled lately. His wife is too busy going nuts to starch his collars.

On top of the stack is an offer for a free manicure at my local mall, as if I give a damn anymore about my nails. In a sudden rage I sweep the mail off the table and it goes flying. An envelope lands on the floor at my feet. An envelope with a Rome postmark. I recognize the sender's name: Anna Maria Padrone.

I snatch it up and rip it open.

Dear Mrs. Ansdell,

I am sorry it has taken me so long to reply, but we have had a terrible tragedy. My grandfather is dead. A few days after I last wrote to you, he was killed during a robbery at the shop. The police are investigating, but we have little hope they will find whoever did this. My family is in mourning, and we wish to be left in peace. I am sorry, but I cannot answer any more of your questions. I ask that you do not call or write me again. Please respect our privacy.

For a long time I sit staring at what Anna Maria has written me. I'm desperate to share this news, but with whom? Not Rob or Val, who already think I'm dangerously obsessed with *Incendio*. Not Dr. Rose, who'll just add this to her evidence list for why I'm crazy.

I pick up the phone and call Gerda.

"Oh my God," she murmurs. "He was *murdered*?"

"It doesn't make any sense to me, Gerda. He had nothing but junk in his shop, old furniture and horrible paintings. There are so many other antiques shops on that street. Why would thieves break into his?"

"Maybe it looked like an easy target. Maybe there were more valuable items you didn't notice."

"Old books and music? That was the most valuable stuff he had. Hardly what a thief would go for." I look down at the letter from Rome. "The granddaughter doesn't want to hear from me again, so I guess we'll never find out where the music comes from."

"There's still a way," says Gerda. "We have that Venice address, written on the back of the book of Gypsy tunes. If the composer once lived there, maybe we could track down his family. What if he's written other music that's never been published? What if we could be the first to record it?"

"Your fantasies are getting ahead of you. We don't even know if he lived there."

"I'll try to find out. I'm packing for Trieste right now. Remember that gig I told you about? Right after it's over, I'm heading to Venice. I've already booked a cute little hotel in Dorsoduro." She pauses. "Why don't you meet me there?"

"In Venice?"

"You've been sounding so depressed lately, Julia. You could use a little escape to Italy. We could solve the mystery of *Incendio* and have a girl's getaway at the same time. What do you think? Can Rob set you free for a week?"

"I wish I *could* go."

"Why can't you?"

Because I'm about to be locked away in the nuthouse and I'll probably never see Italy again.

I look down at the letter and think of the gloomy little shop where I found the music. I remember the gargoyles over the door and the Medusa head knocker. And I remember how chilled I felt, as though I already sensed that Death would soon pay a visit there. Somehow I brought the curse of that place home with me, in the guise of a single sheet of manuscript paper. Even if I burned that music here, now, I don't think I'd ever be able to break free of that curse. I'll never get my daughter back. Certainly not while locked away inside a mental institution.

This could be my only chance to fight back. My only chance to reclaim my family.

My head lifts. "When will you be in Venice?" I ask Gerda.

"The festival in Trieste runs through Sunday. I plan to take the train to Venice on Monday. Why?"

"I've just changed my mind. I'll meet you there."

15

When everyone believes you are being perfectly co-operative, it's a simple matter to escape your life and slip out of the country. I buy my ticket online at Orbitz—*only two more tickets left at this price!*—departing in the late afternoon, arriving in Venice early the next morning. I ask Val to keep Lily at her house while I prepare for my upcoming hospitalization. I listen attentively to everything Rob says, however inane, so he cannot accuse me of hearing imaginary voices while he's talking to me. I cook three excellent dinners in a row, serve them all with a smile, and mention not a word about *Incendio* or Italy.

On the day of my flight, I tell him I'll be at my hairdresser's until five, which, when you think about it, is a ridiculous excuse because why would any woman care how her hair looks when she's about to check in to the loony bin? But Rob thinks this is perfectly reasonable. He won't start to worry about my whereabouts until later in the evening when I don't return home.

By then I am already over the Atlantic Ocean, sitting in row twenty-eight, middle seat, between an elderly Italian woman on my right and a distracted-looking businessman on my left. Neither one wants to chat with me, which is too bad because I'm desperate to talk with someone, anyone, even this pair of strangers. I want to confess that I'm a runaway wife, that I'm scared but also a little thrilled. That I have nothing left to lose because my husband thinks I'm insane and my psychiatrist wants to lock me away. That I've never done anything this crazy and impulsive, and it feels strangely wonderful. It feels like the *real* Julia has broken out of prison, and she has a mission to complete. A mission to reclaim her daughter and her life.

The flight attendants dim the cabin lights and everyone around me nestles down to sleep, but I sit wide awake, thinking about what must be happening at home. Rob will surely call Val and Dr. Rose, and then he'll call the police. *My crazy wife has disappeared.* He won't know right away that I've left the country. Only Gerda knows where I'm headed, and she's already in Italy.

While I have been to Rome several times, I have visited Venice only once before, when Rob and I were on vacation four years ago. It was in August, and I remember the city as a confusing maze of alleys and bridges overrun with tourists packed skin to clammy skin. I remember the smell of sweat and seafood and sunscreen. And I remember the white-hot glare of the sun.

Once again, that sun is glaring down as I walk out of the airport, dazed and blinking. Yes, this is the Venice I remember. Only it's even more crowded—and much more expensive.

I blow almost my entire stash of euros on a private water taxi ride to the neighborhood of Dorsoduro, where Gerda has booked a room in a small hotel. Tucked into a quiet alley, the modest establishment has a dark lobby with worn velvet chairs and the sort of local character that she would call charming, but which I find merely shabby. Although she hasn't yet checked in, our room is ready and the twin beds look clean and inviting. I'm so exhausted I don't even bother to shower, but collapse on top of the sheets. In seconds, I am asleep.

"Julia." A hand nudges me. "Hey, are you ever going to wake up?"

I open my eyes and see Gerda bending over me. She looks bright and cheerful—too cheerful, I think, as I groan and stretch.

"I think I've let you sleep long enough. It really is time for you to wake up."

"When did you get here?"

"Hours ago. I've already been out for a walk and had lunch. It's three o'clock."

"I didn't sleep at all on the plane."

"If you don't get up soon, you won't sleep a wink tonight. Come on, or you'll never get over jet lag."

As I sit up, I hear my cellphone vibrate on the nightstand.

"It's done that about half a dozen times now,"
she says.

"I turned off the ringer so I could sleep."

"Maybe you should check your messages. It
sounds like someone really wants to reach you."

I pick up the phone and scroll through the half-
dozen missed calls and text messages. Rob, Rob,
Rob, Val, Rob. I drop the phone into my purse.
"Nothing important. Just Rob checking in."

"Was he okay with you coming to Venice?"

I shrug. "He'll understand. If he calls you, don't
bother to answer. He'll just give you grief about my
being here."

"You did tell him you were coming to Venice,
didn't you?"

"I told him I needed to get away for a while,
that's all. I said I was going on a girls' holiday and
I'll come home when I'm good and rested." I see
her frowning at me and I add: "There's nothing to
worry about. I've got a long way before I max out
my credit card."

"It's not your credit card that concerns me. I'm
worried about you and Rob. This isn't like you, to
leave without telling him where you're going."

"You did invite me here, remember?"

"Yes, but I didn't expect you to jump on a plane
without first discussing it with him." She studies
me. "Do you want to talk about it?"

I avoid her gaze and turn to look out the window.
"He doesn't believe me, Gerda. He thinks I'm delusional."

"About the music, you mean?"

"He doesn't understand its power. He certainly

wouldn't understand why I've come all this way to track down the composer. He'd call this trip crazy."

Gerda sighs. "I guess I must be crazy, too, because I'm here looking for the same answers."

"Then we should get started." I pick up my purse and sling it over my shoulder. "Let's go find Calle del Forno."

We soon discover there is more than one Calle del Forno in Venice. The first one we visit is in the *sestiere* of Santa Croce, where at 4 P.M. the alleys are thronged with tourists browsing the little shops and wine bars near the Rialto Bridge. Even this late in the day the heat is stifling and my head is still fogged from jet lag. We cannot find the address No. 11, so we stop at a gelato shop, where Gerda struggles to communicate in her rudimentary Italian with the middle-aged woman behind the counter. The woman looks at the written address, shakes her head, and calls out to a skinny teenage boy who sits slouched at a corner table.

Scowling, the boy pulls off his iPod earbuds and says to us in English, "My mother says you are on the wrong street."

"But this *is* Calle del Forno, isn't it?" Gerda hands the boy the written address. "We can't find number eleven."

"There is no number eleven on this street. You want Calle del Forno in Cannaregio. A different *sestiere*."

"Is that neighborhood very far?"

He shrugs. "You cross at Ponte degli Scalzi. Walk five, maybe ten minutes."

"Could you take us there?"

The teenager flashes her a *why would I do that?* look that needs no translation. Only when Gerda offers to pay him twenty euros to take us there does his face brighten. He shoves to his feet and stuffs the iPod in his pocket. "I show you."

The boy leads us at a trot through tourist-packed streets, his red T-shirt weaving in and out of sight. Once, after he darts around a corner, we lose sight of him entirely. Then we hear a shout of "Hey! Ladies!" and spot him waving far ahead of us. The boy intends to waste no time collecting those twenty euros, and he keeps urging us forward, impatient with these slow-poke Americans who keep getting hung up in the thronged alleys.

On the other side of Ponte degli Scalzi, the crowds grow even thicker and we're helplessly swept along in the river of travelers spilling out of the nearby train station. By now I've given up trying to remember our route, and I register only what leaps out at me from the swirl of color and noise. The girl with the sunburned face. A shop window with leering Carnevale masks. A bull-sized man in a tank top, his shoulders bristling with hair. Then the boy veers from the canal, and the crowds thin away to nothing. We are alone as we turn down a gloomy passage where crumbling buildings squeeze ever closer, as if leaning in to crush us.

The boy points. "Here. This is number eleven."

I stare up at flaking paint and sagging walls, at a façade webbed with cracks, like wrinkles on an ancient face. Through the dusty windows, I see empty rooms littered with cardboard boxes and crumpled newspapers.

"This place looks like it's been abandoned for some time," says Gerda. She scans the alley and sees two elderly women watching us from a doorway. "Ask those ladies who owns this building," she commands the boy.

"You promised me twenty euros to bring you here."

"Okay, okay." Gerda hands him the money. "Now, could you please just ask them the question?"

The teenager calls out to the elderly women. This leads to a noisy conversation shouted in Italian. The women leave their doorway and approach us. One has an eye that's milky from a cataract; the other walks with a cane, grasped in a hand that's grotesquely deformed by arthritis.

"They say an American man bought the building last year," the boy tells us. "He wants to make an art gallery."

Both old women snort at the absurdity of yet another gallery in Venice, where the city itself is a living, breathing work of art.

"Before the American bought it, who lived here?" Gerda asks.

The boy points to the arthritic woman with the cane. "She says her family owned it for many years. Her father bought it, after the war."

I reach into my shoulder bag for the book of Gypsy music. From its pages I pull out the single sheet with *Incendio* and point to the composer's name. "Has she ever heard of this person, L. Todesco?"

The woman with the arthritic hands bends closer and stares at the name. For a long time she says nothing. Reaching out, she gently touches the page and murmurs in Italian.

"What is she saying?" I ask the boy.

"She says they went away and never came back."

"Who?"

"The people who lived in this building. Before the war."

Gnarled fingers suddenly grasp my arm and tug, urging me to follow. Down the alley the woman leads us, her cane thunking against the pavement. Despite her age and infirmity, she moves at a determined pace around the corner, into a busier street. I realize the boy's taken off and abandoned us, so we can't ask the woman where we're going. Perhaps she's misunderstood our request and we'll end up in her family's trinket shop. She takes us over a bridge, across a town square, and points a crooked finger at a wall.

Engraved on wood panels is a continuous series of names and numbers: ... GILMO PERLMUTTER 45 BRUNO PERLMUTTER 9 LINA PRANI CORINALDI 71 ...

"*Qui,*" the woman says softly. "Lorenzo."

It's Gerda who spots it first. "Oh my God, Julia," she gasps. "There he is!" She points to the name, engraved among the others: LORENZO TODESCO 24.

The old woman looks at me with haunted eyes and whispers: "*L'ultimo treno.*"

"Julia, this is some sort of memorial plaque,"

Gerda says. "If I understand it correctly, it explains what happened here, in this square."

Although the words are Italian, their meaning is clear even to me. *Ebraica. Deportati. Fascisti dai nazisti.* Two hundred and forty-six Italian Jews, deported from this city. Among them was a young man named Lorenzo Todesco.

I glance around the square and spot the words *Campo Ghetto Nuovo.* Now I know where we are: the Jewish quarter. I cross the square to a different building, where there are bronze plaques showing scenes of deportation and concentration camps, and I focus on the image of a train spilling out its cargo of doomed human beings. *L'ultimo treno,* the old woman told us. The last train, which took away the family that once lived at No. 11, Calle del Forno.

My head throbs in the heat and I feel dizzy. "I need to sit down," I tell Gerda. I make my way to the shade of an enormous tree and sink onto the public bench. There I sit massaging my scalp, thinking about Lorenzo Todesco, only twenty-four years old. So young. His home in that now-derelict building on Calle del Forno stands only a few hundred paces from where I now sit. Perhaps he once rested under this same tree, walked across these same paving stones. Perhaps I'm now sitting in the very same spot where the melody of *Incendio* came to him as he contemplated his grim future.

"The Jewish Museum is right over there," Gerda says, pointing to a nearby building. "Someone in there must speak English. Let me ask them if they know anything about the Todesco family."

While Gerda heads into the museum, I remain on the bench, my head buzzing as if a million bees are swarming in my brain. Tourists wander past, but it's only the bees I hear, drowning out the voices and footfalls. I cannot stop thinking about Lorenzo, who was nine years younger than I am now. I think about where I was nine years ago. A newlywed with a whole life ahead of me. I had a comfortable home, a career I loved, and no dark clouds on my horizon. But for Lorenzo, a Jew in a world gone mad, dark clouds were rapidly closing in.

"Julia?" Gerda has returned. Beside her stands a pretty, dark-haired young woman. "This is Francesca, a curator from the Jewish Museum. I told her why we're here. She'd like to see *Incendio*."

I pull the music from my shoulder bag and give it to the young woman, who frowns at the name of the composer. "You bought this in Rome?" she asks me.

"I found it in an antiques shop. I paid a hundred euros for it," I add sheepishly.

"This paper does appear to be old," Francesca concedes. "But I doubt this composer was from the same Todesco family who lived here in Cannaregio."

"So you've heard of that Todesco family?"

She nods. "We have files on all the Jewish deportees in our archives. Bruno Todesco was a well-known luthier in Venice. I believe he had two sons and a daughter. I'll have to review the files, but they may have lived on Calle del Forno."

"Couldn't this composer L. Todesco be one of his sons? That waltz was tucked into an old music book with the Calle del Forno address written on it."

Francesca shakes her head. "All the family's books and papers were burned by the fascists. As far as we know, nothing survived. If the Todescos managed to save anything from the fire, it was later lost in the death camp where they were sent. So this composition . . ." Francesca holds up *Incendio*. "Should not even exist."

"But it does," I say. "And I paid a hundred euros for it."

She is still studying the music. She holds it up to the sunlight and squints at the penciled notes on the staves. "This antiques store in Rome, did they tell you where they obtained the music?"

"The dealer bought it from the estate of a man named Capobianco."

"Capobianco?"

"That's what the shopkeeper's granddaughter wrote me." I reach into my shoulder bag again, take out the letters from Anna Maria Padrone, and hand them to Francesca. "Mr. Capobianco lived in the town of Casperia. I believe it's not far from Rome."

She reads the first letter, then unfolds the second. Suddenly I hear her suck in a sharp breath and when she looks at me, something has changed in her eyes. The spark of interest has been lit, a fire started. "This antiques dealer was murdered?"

"Only a few weeks ago. There was a robbery at his shop."

She focuses again on *Incendio*. She's now holding it gingerly, as if the paper has transformed into something dangerous. Something too scorching to hold in her bare hands. "May I keep this music for a while? I want my people to examine it. And these letters, too."

"Your people?"

"Our document scholars. I assure you, they will take very good care of it. If this music is as old as it appears, it should not be touched anymore by human hands. Let me know which hotel you're staying in, and I'll call you tomorrow."

"We do have copies of the music at home," Gerda says to me. "There's no reason we can't let her borrow it for a proper examination."

I look at *Incendio* and think of how that lone sheet of paper has brought such misery to my life. How it has fractured my family and poisoned my love for my daughter.

"Take it," I say. "I never want to see the bloody thing again."

I should feel relieved that *Incendio* is no longer my burden, that it's now in the hands of people who will know what to do with it, yet that night I lie awake, fretting about all the unanswered questions. As Gerda sleeps soundly in the next bed, I stare at the darkness, wondering if Francesca will track down the music's origins as she promised. Or will it end up as just another document stored in the museum's vault, left for some future scholar to ponder?

I give up on sleep, get dressed in the dark, and slip out of the room.

The lobby desk is manned by a night clerk who looks up from the paperback novel she's reading and gives me a friendly nod. Laughter and loud voices filter in from the street outside; at 1 A.M., the sleepless are still out and about in Venice.

But wandering the city is not what I have in mind tonight. Instead, I approach the night clerk and ask: "Could you help me? I need to reach some people in another town, but I don't know the phone number. Do you have a directory where I can look it up?"

"Of course. Where do they live?"

"A town called Casperia. I think it's close to Rome. Their last name is Capobianco."

The clerk turns to her computer and searches what I assume is the Italian version of the White Pages. "There are two listings for that surname. Filippo Capobianco and Davide Capobianco. Which one do you want?"

"I don't know."

She turns to me with a puzzled look. "You don't know the given name?"

"I just know the family is in Casperia."

"Then I will write down both phone numbers for you." She jots the information on a scrap of paper and hands it to me.

"Could you perhaps . . ."

"Yes?"

"They may not speak English, so I don't know if I'll even be able to talk to them. Could you call them for me?"

"But it is one in the morning, madam."

"No, I mean tomorrow. If there are long-distance

charges, I'll pay whatever it costs. Could you give them a message?"

The woman reaches for a fresh sheet of paper. "What is the message?"

"Tell them my name is Julia Ansdell. I'm looking for the family of Giovanni Capobianco. It's about a piece of music he once owned, by a composer named Lorenzo Todesco."

She scribbles down the message and glances up. "You wish me to call both of the numbers?"

"Yes. I want to be sure I find the right family."

"And if they wish to speak to you? How long will you be a guest here, so I can give you the message?"

"I'm staying another two days." I reach for her pen and write down my cellphone number and email address. "After that, they can reach me in the United States."

The clerk tapes the note to the desk beside the telephone. "I will call in the morning, before I leave."

I know it's a strange request, and I wonder if she'll actually follow through. I have no chance to ask her, because when I stop at the desk the next morning, a different woman is sitting there and the note is no longer taped beside the telephone. No one has left any messages for me. No one except Rob has tried to call my cellphone.

I stand there in the lobby, scrolling through Rob's latest text messages, which were sent at midnight, 2 A.M., and 5 A.M., Boston time. Poor Rob; he is getting no sleep, and it's my fault. I think of the night I was in labor with Lily, and how Rob sat by my bed the whole time, holding my hand, pressing cool washcloths to my forehead. I remember his bleary eyes and unshaven face, and I imagine that's how he looks now. I owe him some sort of answer, so I respond with one short message: *Please don't worry. I need to do this, and then I'll come home.* I press Send, and imagine his look of relief when he sees my words pop up on his cellphone. Or will it be a look of irritation? Am I still the woman he loves, or am I merely the problem in his life?

"There you are, Julia," says Gerda, who's just emerged from the breakfast room. She notices the phone in my hand. "Have you spoken to Rob?"

"I sent him a text."

"Good." She sounds strangely relieved and says again, with a sigh: "Good."

"Have you heard from Francesca? About the music?"

"It's too soon. Give her some time. Meanwhile, I think we should take a walk around this gorgeous city. What do you want to see?"

"I'd like to go back to Cannaregio. The Ghetto Nuovo."

Gerda hesitates, clearly uninterested in returning to the Jewish quarter. "Why don't we go to San Marco first?" she suggests. "I want to do a little shopping and sip Bellinis. We *are* in Venice. Let's be tourists."

And that's exactly how we spend most of the day. We poke around shops in San Marco, squeeze in among the hordes visiting the Doge's Palace, and bargain for trinkets I really don't want on the busy Rialto Bridge.

By the time we finally cross the footbridge into Cannaregio, it is late afternoon and I'm sick of fighting my way through crowds. We escape into the relative quiet of the Jewish quarter, where the narrow streets are already cast in evening shadow. I'm so relieved to be away from the throngs that at first, the silence of the neighborhood doesn't bother me.

But halfway down an alleyway, I suddenly stop and turn to look behind us. I see no one, only a gloomy passage and laundry fluttering on a line high above. There is nothing alarming, yet my skin prickles and my senses are instantly on high alert.

"What is it?" Gerda asks.

"I thought I heard someone behind us."

"I don't see anyone."

I can't stop scanning the alley, searching for a flicker of movement. I see only the laundry swaying overhead, three faded shirts and a towel.

"No one's there. Come on," she says and keeps walking.

I have no choice but to follow her, because I don't want to be left alone in that claustrophobic passage. We make our way back to the Campo Ghetto Nuovo, where once again I'm drawn to the plaque with the names of deported Jews. There he is, Lorenzo Todesco. While Francesca has her doubts he is the composer, I feel certain that *Incendio* is his. Seeing his name carved here is like coming face-to-face with someone I have known for a long time, but only now am able to recognize.

"It's late," says Gerda. "Shall we head back?"

"Not yet." I cross the square to the Jewish Museum, which has already closed for the day. Through the window, I spy a man inside, straightening up a stack of pamphlets. I rap on the glass and he shakes his head and points to his watch. When I knock again, he finally unlocks the door and regards me with a *go away* scowl.

"Is Francesca here?" I ask.

"She left this afternoon. To see a journalist."

"Will she be here tomorrow?"

"I don't know. Come back then." With that, he shuts the door, and I hear the angry clunk of the bolt sliding home.

That night Gerda and I dine in a mediocre restaurant that we choose at random, one of the countless pizza and pasta traps near Piazza San Marco that cater to tourists who will never return. Every table is taken and we sit elbow-to-elbow with a family of sunburned Midwesterners who laugh too loud and drink too much. I have no appetite, and I have to force myself to eat the tasteless spaghetti Bolognese that sprawls like a bloody thing across my plate.

Gerda sounds far too upbeat as she refills her glass of Chianti from the carafe. "I'd say we accomplished our mission, Julia. We came, we asked, we got an answer. Now we know who our composer was."

"Francesca sounded doubtful."

"The name fits, the address fits. It must be Lorenzo Todesco's. It sounds like the family's all dead, so I think we're safe recording the piece.

When we get home, let's get to work on a quartet arrangement. I'm sure Stephanie can come up with some lovely harmony on the cello."

"I don't know, Gerda. It feels wrong, recording this waltz."

"What's wrong about it?"

"It's like we're exploiting him. Profiting from his tragedy. There's such an awful history to this music, I wonder if we're asking for bad luck."

"Julia, it's only a waltz."

"And the man who sold me that waltz gets murdered in Rome. It's as if the music leaves a curse on everyone who touches it or hears it. Even my own daughter."

Gerda is silent for a moment. She takes a sip of wine and calmly sets down the goblet. "Julia, I know it's been rough for you these past few weeks. The problems with Lily. Your fall down the stairs. But I don't think that has anything to do with *Incendio*. Yes, the music is disturbing. It's complex and powerful and it comes with a tragic history. But it's just notes on a page, and those notes need to be heard. That's the way we honor Lorenzo Todesco, by sharing his music with the world. It gives him the immortality he deserves."

"What about my daughter?"

"What about Lily?"

"The music changed her. I know it did."

"Maybe it just seems that way. When things go wrong, it's natural to look for an explanation, but there may not be one." She reaches across the table and places her hand on mine. "Go home, Julia.

Talk to Rob. You two need to sort this out together."

I look straight at her, but she avoids my gaze.
Why has everything suddenly changed between us?
If even Gerda has turned against me, I'm left with
no one on my side.

We are silent as we leave the restaurant and walk
across the Accademia Bridge, back to the neighborhood of Dorsoduro. Despite the late hour, the
streets are alive and throbbing with noise. It's a
warm night and the hip young set is everywhere,
loud boys with untucked shirts, carefree girls in
short skirts and halter tops, flirting, laughing,
drinking. But Gerda and I don't exchange a word
as we veer away from that busy street and turn
down a far quieter alley, toward our hotel.

By now Rob probably knows I'm in Venice. A
look at our online accounts would tell him I've
withdrawn cash at a Venice ATM and I've just used
my credit card at a restaurant in San Marco. There's
no way to keep those kinds of secrets from an accountant; he's an expert at following the money. I
feel guilty not returning any of his phone calls, but
I'm afraid of what he'll say to me. I dread hearing
him tell me that he's reached his limit. After ten
years of marriage, a good marriage, is it possible
I've lost him?

At the far end of the alley is the faint glow of our
hotel sign. As we approach it, I'm still thinking
about Rob, about what I will say to him and how
we can survive this. I don't notice the man standing
in the doorway. Then a silhouette, broad-shouldered
and faceless, suddenly detaches itself from the

shadows and moves in front of us, blocking our way.

"Julia Ansdell?" he asks. Deep voice, Italian accent.

Gerda says: "Who are you?"

"I am looking for Mrs. Ansdell."

"Well, this is entirely the wrong way to go about it," Gerda snaps. "Are you *trying* to scare her?"

As the man moves toward us, I back away until I'm pressed against a wall. "Stop it, you're freaking her out!" says Gerda. "Her husband didn't say it would be done this way!"

Her husband. With those two words, everything becomes shockingly clear. I look at Gerda. "You—Rob—"

"Julia, honey, he called me this morning, while you were still asleep. He explained everything. Your breakdown, the psychiatrist. They're trying to get you home to the hospital. He promised not to upset you, but then he sends *this* asshole." She steps between me and the man and pushes him away from me. "Back off now, you hear me? If her husband wants her home, he'll just have to come here himself and—"

The gunshot makes me freeze. Gerda stumbles against me and I try to hold her up, but she crumples to the ground. I feel her blood, warm and wet, streak down my arms.

Suddenly the hotel door swings open and I hear two men laughing as they step out of the building. The gunman turns toward them, momentarily distracted.

That's when I run.

I sprint instinctively toward lights, toward the safety of crowds. I hear another gunshot, feel air whistle past my cheek. I dart around the corner and see a café ahead and people dining at outdoor tables. As I race toward them, I try to scream to them to help me, but panic has made my throat close over and almost no sound comes out. I'm certain the man is right behind me so I keep running. People glance up as I tear past them. More eyes, more witnesses, but who is going to stand between me and a bullet?

The Accademia Bridge is the most direct way out of Dorsoduro. Once across it, I can join the larger crowds in San Marco, lose myself in those eternally celebrating throngs. And I remember seeing a police station there.

The bridge is just ahead. My passage to safety.

I'm only a few paces across it when a hand grabs me, yanks me to a halt. Whirling around, I'm ready to scratch at my attacker's eyes, ready to fight for my life, but the face I see is a young woman's. It is Francesca from the Jewish Museum.

"Mrs. Ansdell, we were just on our way to see you." She pauses, frowning at my panicked face. "What's wrong? Why are you running?"

I glance back, frantically scanning faces. "There's a man—he's trying to kill me!"

"What?"

"He was waiting at the hotel. Gerda—my friend Gerda—" My voice cracks into a sob. "I think she's dead."

Francesca turns and speaks in Italian to a bearded young man who's standing beside her. With his backpack and scholarly spectacles, he looks like some earnest graduate student. The man gives a grim nod and hurries off in the direction of my hotel.

"My colleague Salvatore will see what happened to your friend," she says. "Now quickly, come with me. We need to get you out of sight."

Lorenzo ❧

16

December 1943

When you cannot see where you are going, when you do not know your final destination, every hour is its own eternity.

Night had fallen, and with all the shades closed, Lorenzo could no longer tell in which direction their train was moving. He imagined fields and farmlands beyond the window, small villages where lights glowed in houses and families sat at supper tables. Did they hear the faint clack of the train passing by? Did they pause, forks halfway to their mouths, and wonder about the people aboard the train? Or did they simply continue with their suppers, because what went on beyond their walls was none of their concern, and what could they do about it anyway? This train, like all those before it, would move on, so they break bread and drink wine and carry on with their lives. *While we pass by like ghosts in the night.*

His arm had gone numb, but he didn't want to move it because Pia had fallen asleep with her head on his shoulder. She had not bathed in days, and her long hair was clumped and greasy. How proud she was of her hair, how she liked to stroke it back over her shoulders whenever a fine-looking boy passed by. Would any boy look at her now, with her hair dull and stringy, her face so thin and pale? Her long lashes cast shadows that looked like bruises under her eyes. He pictured her toiling in a work camp, shivering in the cold, growing ever thinner and weaker. He kissed the top of her head, and instead of her usual fragrance of rose water, he smelled sweat and dirty scalp. How quickly humans are reduced to wretchedness, he thought. Only a few days without food or beds or baths, and the fire has gone out in us all, even Marco, who now sat slumped in despair.

The train suddenly lurched and ground to a stop. Through the closed shades, he saw the cold glare of platform lights.

Pia jerked awake and looked up at him with drowsy eyes. "Are we there? Is this Fossoli?"

"I don't know, darling."

"I'm so hungry. Why don't they feed us? It's wrong to make us go so long without food."

The train doors squealed open and voices shouted: *"Alle runter! Alle runter!"*

"What are they saying?" Pia's voice rose in fear. "I don't understand what they want us to do!"

"They're ordering us to get off the train," said Marco.

"Then we must do what they tell us." Lorenzo picked up his violin and said to Pia, "Stay close to me, dearest. Hold my hand."

"Mama?" Pia called out in panic. "Papa?"

"Everything will be fine, I'm sure of it," said Bruno. "Just don't call attention to yourself, don't look at anyone. We must simply get through this." Their father managed a weak smile. "And we must stay together. That's the most important thing. Stay together."

Pia kept her head down, her hand in Lorenzo's as they shuffled off the train behind Mama and Papa and Marco. Outside it was so cold that their breaths steamed and swirled in the air. Floodlights shone down on the train platform, bright as day, and the detainees squinted, confused in the glare as they huddled together to stay warm. Pressed in on all sides, jostled by the crowd, Lorenzo and his sister were two lost swimmers in a sea of frightened souls. Behind him a baby screamed so loudly that he could not hear the orders shouted from the far end of the platform. Only when a guard stepped forward and began shoving people apart did he understand that they were to line up for inspection. As they shivered side by side, Pia continued to cling to his hand, afraid to be set adrift. Lorenzo glanced at Marco, standing to his right, but his brother faced straight ahead, chin jutting out and shoulders squared, as if daring the guards to intimidate him.

As soldiers paced closer, moving down the line of prisoners, Lorenzo stared down at the platform. He saw a pair of polished boots suddenly halt in front of him.

"You," a voice said.

Slowly Lorenzo lifted his eyes to see an SS officer staring at him. The officer asked a question in German. Lorenzo could not understand and shook his head in bewilderment. The officer pointed to the violin Lorenzo was holding. Asked the question again.

An Italian guard stepped forward to translate. "He wants to know if the instrument is yours."

Terrified that they were going to confiscate La Dianora, Lorenzo's grip tightened on the case. "Yes, it's mine."

"Do you play this violin?"

Lorenzo swallowed. "Yes."

"What sort of music do you play?"

"Any music. Whatever is put before me."

The Italian guard looked at the German officer, who gave a brusque nod.

"You will come with us," the Italian said.

"My family as well?"

"No. Only you."

"But I must stay with my family."

"We have no use for them." He waved to two soldiers who stepped forward and took Lorenzo by both arms.

"No. *No.*"

"Lorenzo!" Pia screamed as he was torn from her grasp. "Don't take him! Please don't take him!"

He twisted around, trying to catch a final glimpse of her. He saw Pia struggling against Marco, who restrained her. He saw his mother and father clinging to each other in despair. Then he was dragged down a set of concrete steps and marched away from the platform. Still blinded by the glare of the floodlights, he could not see where he was going, but he could hear Pia screaming his name.

"My family—please let me stay with my family!" he begged.

One of the soldiers snorted. "You don't want to go where they're going."

"Where are they going?"

"Let's just say you're the lucky one, you idiot."

Pia's cries faded behind him as Lorenzo was marched down a rutted road. Away from the lights, he could now make out the high walls ahead of him. Against the night sky, ominous towers loomed like stone giants and he felt guards' eyes staring down as he was marched through the gate. They crossed the courtyard to a low-slung building, and one of his escorts gave three hard knocks on a door.

A voice inside commanded them to enter.

Shoved from behind, Lorenzo tripped over the threshold and almost dropped La Dianora as he stumbled into the room. Crouched on the floor, he smelled cigarettes and wood smoke. Heard the door slam shut behind him.

"Imbeciles!" a voice barked in Italian. The insult was not directed at Lorenzo but at the two soldiers. "You can see he's carrying a violin, can't you? I'll have your hides if it's damaged!"

Slowly Lorenzo rose to his feet, but he was too terrified to focus on the man who'd spoken. Instead he looked everywhere else. He saw scuffed wood floors, a table and chairs, an ashtray filled with cigarette butts. A single lamp burned on a desk, where papers were arranged in four orderly stacks.

"What do we have here? Look at me."

At last Lorenzo's gaze lifted to the man, and suddenly he could not look anywhere else. He saw brilliant blue eyes, a startling contrast to the man's coal-black hair. Those eyes stared with such intensity that Lorenzo felt pierced to the spot. In every way this man radiated power, and on his uniform he wore his chilly insignia of authority. He was Italian SS. A colonel.

One of the soldiers said, "This man claims he's a musician."

"And the violin?" The Colonel glanced at the instrument case. "Is it in any condition to be played?" His gaze snapped back to Lorenzo. "Well, is it?"

Lorenzo took in a shaky breath. "Yes. Sir."

"Open it." The Colonel gestured to the table. "Let's take a look."

Lorenzo set the case down on the table. Hands chilled and fumbling, he undid the latches and lifted the lid. Inside, La Dianora gleamed like polished amber, a jewel cradled in black velvet.

The Colonel gave a murmur of admiration. "And how did you come by this instrument?"

"It was my grandfather's. And before that, his grandfather's."

"You say you're a musician?"

"Yes."

"Prove it. Let me hear you play."

Lorenzo's hands were stiff from cold and fear. He squeezed his fists to pump warming blood into his fingers before he lifted La Dianora from her velvet bed. Despite the long train ride and the cold platform, she was still in tune. "What would you like me to play, sir?"

"Anything. Just prove to me that you can."

Lorenzo hesitated. What to play? He was paralyzed by indecision. Trembling, he lifted the bow to the strings and held it there, willing his hands to steady. The seconds ticked by. The Colonel waited. When the bow at last began to move, it was almost of its own volition, as if La Dianora could no longer wait for him to choose the music. A few weak notes, a few hesitant bow strokes, and suddenly the melody burst forth in full-throated song. It poured into every dark corner of that room. It made the air hum and the cigarette smoke dance in the shadows. He needed no sheet music to play this piece; it was permanently engraved in his memory and in his heart.

It was the same music that he and Laura had performed at Ca' Foscari, the duet that would always remind him of the happiest moments of his life. As he played, he could feel her spirit beside him, could remember the black satin dress she wore onstage that night and the curve of her shoulders as she embraced her cello. How her hair slid away to reveal a delicious glimpse of the nape of her neck. He played as if she were seated beside him. He closed his eyes and suddenly everything vanished but Laura. He forgot where he was, forgot his weariness and his hunger and his fear. Laura was his strength, the elixir that breathed life into his stiff hands, and every note he played was his heart calling out to hers across time, across the desolate miles that separated them. His body swayed to the music, sweat beading on his forehead. The room that had at first seemed so cold now felt like a furnace and he was burning up in it, consumed by the fire that sizzled from the strings. *Are you listening, my darling? Can you hear me singing to you?*

His bow came down on the final note. As it faded, the chill of the room seeped back into his limbs. Exhausted, he lowered the bow and stood with head down and shoulders slumped.

For a long moment, no one spoke.

Then the Colonel said: "I am unfamiliar with this piece. Who is the composer?"

"I am," Lorenzo murmured.

"Indeed? *You* composed this music?"

Lorenzo gave a weary nod. "It is a duet for violin and cello."

"So you are able to write for ensembles."

"If the inspiration strikes me."

"I see. I see." The Colonel paced a circle around him, as if to inspect him from all angles. Abruptly he turned to the two soldiers. "Leave us."

"Should we wait outside, sir? You can't predict what he might—"

"What, you think I can't deal with one pathetic prisoner? Yes, stand outside if you wish. But leave." The Colonel waited, stone-faced and silent, until the men retreated from the room. Only when the door swung shut did he focus once again on Lorenzo. "Sit," he commanded.

Lorenzo placed his violin back in the case and he sank into a chair, so sapped by his performance that his legs could not have supported him much longer.

The Colonel picked up La Dianora and held her to the lamplight, admiring her warm patina. "In the hands of someone less skillful, an instrument like this would be wasted. But in your hands, she comes to life." He lifted the violin to his ear and tapped the back, listening to the rich resonance of the wood. As he set La Dianora back in the case, he spotted the collection of Gypsy music tucked inside the lid. He pulled out the book and frowned as he flipped through the pages.

Lorenzo's stomach tightened into a knot. Had the book been a collection of works by an esteemed composer such as Mozart or Bach or Schubert, he would not be apprehensive, but these were Roma tunes, the music of untouchables. He watched as the Colonel slid the music back into the case.

"It's from my grandfather's library," Lorenzo quickly explained. "He is a music professor at Ca' Foscari. It's his job to collect all manner of—"

"About music, I choose not to pass judgment," said the Colonel with a wave of absolution. "I'm not like these Blackshirt thugs who burn books and smash instruments. No, I appreciate music, all music. Even in the midst of this nasty business, we mustn't lose our appreciation for art, don't you agree?" Lips pursed, he studied Lorenzo for a moment. He crossed to the sideboard and returned with the meager remains of his supper, which he set in front of Lorenzo.

"An artist needs fuel before he can create. Eat," he urged.

Lorenzo stared down at a crust of bread and congealed gravy cloaked in a white layer of fat. There was no meat left, only a few lumps of carrot and onion, but to a famished man, this was a feast. Yet he did not touch it. He pictured his sister's thin face. He thought of his mother, weak and unsteady from hunger.

"My family hasn't eaten all day," he said. "No one on the train has eaten. Could you not give them—"

"Do you want it or not?" the Colonel snapped. "Because if you don't, I'll feed it to the dogs."

Lorenzo picked up the bread and held it for a moment, haunted by guilt, but too hungry to resist it. He scraped it through the gravy, scooping up a slimy ribbon of grease, and crammed it into his mouth, sighing as the flavors exploded on his tongue. Silky beef fat. The sweetness of carrots. The yeasty bitterness of burned crust. He dredged the remaining fragment through the gravy, and when the bread was gone, he used his fingers to wipe up the last streak of grease and finally licked the plate.

The Colonel sat in the chair across from him, smoking a cigarette as he watched with an expression that was half amusement, half boredom. "I'll take that away before you start chewing on the chinaware," he said and set the plate back on the sideboard. "I can arrange for more."

"Please. My family is hungry, too."

"You can't change that."

"But *you* can." Lorenzo dared to look the man in the eye. "My sister is only fourteen. Her name is Pia and she's done nothing wrong. She's a good soul, a kind soul, and she deserves to live. And my mother, she's not well, but she'll work hard. They all will."

"There is nothing I can do for them. I advise you to stop thinking about them."

"Stop *thinking* about them? This is my family, and it's not possible for anyone to—"

"It's not just possible, it's *necessary* if you hope to survive. Tell me. Are you a survivor?"

Lorenzo looked into crystal blue eyes, and in that instant he knew that *this* man certainly was a survivor. Drop him in the ocean or throw him into a howling mob and somehow he would find a way to walk away unscathed. Now the Colonel was challenging Lorenzo to do the same, to cast off any and all burdens that could drag him under the waves.

"I want to be with them," Lorenzo said. "Don't separate us. If my family stays together, I know we'll all work harder here. We'll be of far more use to you."

"Where, exactly, do you think you are?"

"We were told we were going to Fossoli."

The Colonel grunted. "You are not in Fossoli. You are in San Sabba. This is merely a transit camp. From here, most deportees are sent elsewhere, unless they fill a special need. Like you."

"Then I must return to the train before it leaves."

"Believe me, you don't want to get back on that train."

"Where are they going? Please tell me where they're going."

The Colonel took a long pull on his cigarette and exhaled. Gazing at Lorenzo through a veil of smoke, he said: "The train goes north. To Poland."

* * *

The Colonel slid a glass of wine in front of Lorenzo. Poured another for himself and took a sip as he regarded the prisoner seated across the table from him. "You're one of the lucky ones. You should be grateful you're staying here at San Sabba."

"My family—where in Poland are they going?"

"It hardly matters."

"It matters to me."

The Colonel shrugged and lit another cigarette. "Whatever camp they end up in, it will be cold there. Colder than you can imagine. That's all I can guarantee."

"My sister has only a thin coat. And she's frail—she can't perform hard labor. If she were assigned to women's work—sewing uniforms or scrubbing pots—she could manage that. Can't it be arranged?"

"You don't understand at all, do you? What it means for a Jew to be sent to Poland? A fate you can escape if you work with me."

"My sister—"

"Forget your bloody sister!"

Lorenzo was shocked by the Colonel's roar. In his desperation to save Pia, he had lost sight of his own perilous position. This man could order him executed on the spot, and judging by the fury in his eyes, he seemed to be considering that very option. The seconds ticked by as Lorenzo sat on the edge of doom, prepared for the punch of a bullet into his head.

The Colonel leaned back in his chair and took another sip of wine. "You know, if you cooperate, you just might survive. But only if you cooperate."

Lorenzo swallowed, his throat still parched from fear. "What must I do?"

"Play music, that's all. As you did for me." The glow of the lamp cast ominous shadows on the Colonel's face and his eyes had the cold gleam of ice. What manner of creature was he? An opportunist, clearly, but that spoke to neither good nor evil. What sort of heart was beating beneath the pressed uniform?

"For whom will I perform?" asked Lorenzo.

"You will play at any occasion for which the Commandant requires music. Now that Risiera di San Sabba is being expanded, there will be a number of such occasions. Last week, half a dozen officers arrived from Berlin. Next month Herr Lambert himself will come to supervise new construction. There will be receptions, dinners. Guests to entertain."

"So I am to play for German officers," said Lorenzo, unable to hide the note of disgust in his voice.

"You would prefer to be marched outside and executed in the courtyard? Because I can certainly accommodate you."

Lorenzo swallowed. "No, sir."

"Then you will perform whenever and wherever Commandant Oberhauser orders it. I've been tasked to identify musicians talented enough to be part of an ensemble. Thus far, you are the third to be chosen. With you, we now have two violinists and a cellist, which is a start. Every train brings fresh candidates. Perhaps in the next group of prisoners, I'll find a clarinet or horn player. We have already amassed enough instruments to furnish a small orchestra."

Confiscated was what he really meant, from the countless unfortunates who'd been stripped of their possessions. Was La Dianora bound for the same fate, to be swept up as one more anonymous violin to be lost in a storeroom of orphaned instruments? He looked at his violin, as fearful as any mother afraid of having her child ripped from her arms.

"Yours *is* an exquisite instrument," said the Colonel, exhaling a cloud of cigarette smoke. "It's far better than any violin in our collection."

"Please. It was my grandfather's."

"Do you think I'd take it from you? Of course you must be the one to play it, because you know it best." The Colonel leaned forward, his face pushing through the veil of smoke to gaze at him with startling clarity. "Like you, I'm an artist. I know what it's like to be surrounded by those who don't appreciate music or literature. The world's gone mad and war has brought the barbarians to power. We must simply put up with them and adjust to the new order of things."

He speaks of adjustment while I am trying just to stay alive. But the Colonel had offered him a small morsel of hope that staying alive was at least a possibility. This man was a fellow Italian; perhaps he'd be more lenient with his own countryman. Perhaps he'd joined the SS merely to align himself with the powerful and was not a true Nazi but a pragmatist. To survive, one must at least appear to side with the winner.

The Colonel rose and picked up a handful of papers from his desk. He placed a sheaf of blank music manuscript paper in front of Lorenzo. "You will be the one to arrange the music for our new ensemble. Since you seem to know your way around a musical score."

"What sort of music do you wish us to play?"

"None of those Gypsy tunes, for God's sake, or the Commandant will have you shot and I'll be sent to the front. No, they prefer their old familiars. Mozart, Bach. I have piano music you can use as a reference. You'll need to arrange parts for whatever musicians we round up."

"You said we have only two violins and a cello. It's hardly an orchestra."

"Then make your second violinist play twice as many notes! For now, you'll have to make do with what we have." The Colonel tossed a pencil at him. "Prove your worth."

Lorenzo looked down at the manuscript paper, where blank staves waited to be filled with notes. Here, at least, was something familiar, something he understood. Music would anchor him, sustain him. In a world gone insane, it was the one thing that would help him hold on to sanity.

"While you are here at San Sabba, you may witness certain . . . unpleasantness. I advise you to see nothing, hear nothing. Say nothing." The Colonel tapped his fingers on the blank manuscript paper. "Focus only on your music. Do your job well, and you just might survive this place."

17

Late at night, lying in his bunk, Lorenzo could hear the screams from Cell No. 1. He never knew who was being tortured. He never saw the victims. He only knew that from night to night, the voices of the tormented kept changing. Sometimes it was a woman's shrieks, sometimes a man's. Sometimes a baritone voice would crack into the girlish sobs of a boy still on the threshold of manhood. If Lorenzo ever dared to peer through the barred door, he might have glimpsed those poor souls as they were dragged into the cell block and led into the first doorway on the left. He had been warned by the Italian Colonel to *see nothing, hear nothing,* but how could he ignore the shrieks issuing from that interrogation cell? The screams might be in Italian or Slovenian or Croatian, but in every language, the meaning was always the same: *I don't know! I can't tell you! Please stop, I beg you to stop!* Some were partisans; some were Resistance fighters. Some were random unfortunates who had no information to share, and were brutalized merely for the pleasure of their torturers.

See nothing. Hear nothing. Say nothing. And you just might survive.

Lorenzo's five cellmates somehow managed to sleep through the nightly screams. In the bunk beneath his, the drummer was snoring with his usual growls and wet rattles. Did the cries of the tortured ever penetrate his sleep? How did he escape so easily into the sanctuary of dreams? While Lorenzo lay awake, the drummer slept on, as did the others. They slept because they were exhausted and weak and because most human beings can learn to endure almost anything, even the cries of the tormented. It was not that their hearts had hardened; it was because they could do nothing about it, and powerlessness leads to its own form of serenity.

Vittorio the cellist sighed and rolled over. Did he dream of his wife and daughters, whom he had last glimpsed on the San Sabba train platform? The same platform where they had all been singled out as musicians and ripped from those they loved? Even now, months later, the wound left by that separation felt as painful to Lorenzo as a fresh amputation. While their families had almost certainly perished, music had kept alive this ensemble of six broken men.

Each had been handpicked by the Italian Colonel. *A poor man's orchestra,* the Colonel had dubbed them, but they served his purpose. There was Shlomo, the rheumy-eyed drummer from Milan, who'd been arrested with his family as they'd tried to cross the border into Switzerland.

There was Emilio, the second violinist, who'd been dragged from a friend's farmhouse near Brescia, a friend who had been summarily executed for hiding a Jew. There was Vittorio, the cellist, arrested in Vicenza, whose hair had magically turned white within weeks of arriving at San Sabba. There was Carlo, the French horn player who had once been fat, and whose loose skin now flopped in pale drapes over his belly. And finally there was Aleks, the viola player, a Slovene musician so talented he could have found a position with any symphony in the world. Instead here he was in their orchestra of the damned, a mere husk of a man who performed with mechanical fingers and empty eyes. Aleks never spoke of his family or of how he came to San Sabba. Lorenzo did not ask.

He had enough nightmares of his own.

In Cell No. 1, the screams rose to a shriek so piercing that Lorenzo clapped his hands over his ears, desperate to shut out the sound. He pressed them there until the screams faded and all he could hear was the whoosh of his own pulse. When at last he dared to pull his hands away from his ears, he heard the familiar squeal of the cell door and the scrape of the prisoner's body being dragged out to the courtyard.

He knew its final destination.

Three months ago, construction had begun in the building across from their cell block. Though he'd been advised to *see nothing, hear nothing,* Lorenzo could hardly be blind to all the trucks hauling materials through the gate and into the compound. Nor could he avoid noticing the construction team

from Berlin, led by a German architect who cease-
lessly paced the compound, issuing orders. At first
none of the musicians knew what was being built;
the work was taking place inside the opposite
building, out of their sight. Lorenzo assumed they
were adding another cell block to house the flood
of new detainees. Every week, so many men,
women, and children arrived by train that they
were sometimes herded into an open courtyard and
spent days shivering and exposed, waiting to be
transported north. Yes, a new cell block made
sense.

Then he began to hear whispers from the prisoners who'd been conscripted into carrying bricks
and mortar into that windowless new structure.
They had seen an underground tunnel leading to
the chimney stack. No, this was not some new cell
block being built, they told him. It was something
else. Something whose purpose they could only
speculate about.

One cold morning in April, Lorenzo saw smoke
curl from that chimney for the first time.

A day later, the prisoners who had labored inside
the building, who had told Lorenzo what they'd
seen inside, were marched from their cell block.
They did not return. The next morning, from that
chimney billowed a singular stench that could not
be escaped. It clung to clothes and hair, swirled up
throats and noses, and was inhaled into lungs. Both
prisoners and guards alike were forced to breathe
in the dead.

*See nothing. Hear nothing. Say nothing. This is
how you survive.*

Everyone closed their ears to the screams from Cell No. 1 and to the executioner's gunshots beyond the walls of the compound. But there was one sound no one could shut out, a sound so horrifying that even the guards would grimace. Some of the executed prisoners delivered to the ovens were not really dead, but merely stunned by what should have been a fatal bullet or blow, and they were thrown into the flames alive. The soldiers would rev their truck engines or goad their dogs into baying, but those distractions were not sufficient to hide the shrieks that occasionally issued from the smoke-belching monster.

To drown out the noise of the dying, San Sabba's little orchestra of the damned was ordered to play music in the courtyard.

And so every morning, Lorenzo and his ensemble dutifully gathered up their instruments and music stands and marched out of the cell block. He'd lost track of how many weeks had passed since his arrival, but over the last month he'd noted the gradual greening of the vines that scrambled up the buildings, and a few weeks ago had seen tiny white flowers pop up in the cracks between the stones. Even at San Sabba, spring had arrived. He imagined wildflowers blooming beyond the walls and barbed wire and hungered for the smell of earth and grass and woods, but here in the compound there was only the stench of truck exhaust and sewage and chimney smoke.

Since dawn, round after round of gunshots had been booming outside the walls. Now the first truck rolled into the compound, weighed down with the harvest from that morning's gunfire. "More logs for the fire," the Italian Colonel announced as the truck pulled into the courtyard to unload its cargo. Fresh rounds of gunfire exploded beyond the walls, and he turned to his orchestra. "Well, what are you waiting for? Begin!"

They did not choose sedate minuets or quiet airs, for the purpose of this music was not to entertain. It was to disguise and distract, and for that they needed loud marches or dance music, played at maximum volume. The Italian Colonel paced the courtyard as they performed, haranguing his musicians to play louder! Louder! "Not merely *forte,* but *fortissimo*! More drums, more brass!"

The French horn blared and the drum thundered. The four string players sawed away as forcefully as they could, until their bow arms trembled, but it was not loud enough. It could never be loud enough to hide the horrors inside the building with the smokestack.

The first truck pulled away; a second one rolled through the gate, so overloaded that it sagged low on its axles. As it bounced across the courtyard, part of its cargo tumbled out through the open canvas flap and landed with a sickening thud on the stones.

Lorenzo stared down at the man's caved-in skull, the naked limbs, the wasted flesh. *More logs for the fire.* The French horn suddenly fell silent, but the drum kept pounding, Shlomo's rhythm unaffected by the sight of the emaciated corpse. Gamely the strings played on as well, but Lorenzo's bow trembled and his notes slid out of tune as his fingers went numb with the horror of what lay at his feet.

"Play!" The Colonel gave the French horn player a sharp slap on the back of the head. "I order you, *play*!"

After a few tentative honks on his horn, Carlo regained his breath control and now they were all playing again, but not loudly enough to satisfy the Colonel. He paced back and forth, once again chanting "Forte, forte, *forte*!" Lorenzo dug his bow harder into the strings and tried to stay focused on his music stand, but the corpse was staring up at him, and Lorenzo could see that the eyes were green.

Two soldiers jumped out of the truck to retrieve their lost bit of cargo. One of the soldiers tossed down the stub of the cigarette he'd been smoking, crushed it with his boot, and bent down to grasp the dead man's ankles. His partner grasped the wrists and together they swung the corpse back into the truck, as casually as if they were tossing a sack of flour. For them, a dead body tumbling from their vehicle was not even worth a pause in their conversation. And why would it be, when there were so many trucks like theirs rumbling in, day after day, each with the same terrible cargo? The butcher who hacks and saws away at countless carcasses does not think of sweet-faced lambs; he sees only meat. Just as the soldiers delivering their daily load of corpses saw only fresh fuel for the incinerator.

And through it all, the little San Sabba orchestra kept playing. Through the roar of the trucks and

the barking of dogs and the staccato of distant gunfire. Through the screams inside the oven. Most
important, the screams. They played until those
screams at last faded, until the trucks rumbled
away empty and foul-smelling smoke billowed
from the chimney. They played so they would not
have to listen or think or feel, focusing on the music
and only the music. Stick to the tempo! Stay together! Are we still in tune? Don't concern your-
selves with what's happening in that building. Just
keep your eyes on the notes, your bow on the
strings.

And when the day's ordeal was over, when they
were finally given leave to stop playing, they were
too exhausted to rise from their chairs. They sat
with instruments lowered, heads bowed, until the
guards prodded them to their feet. Then back to
their cell they marched in silence. Their instruments
had already spoken for them, and there was nothing left to say.

Until nightfall, when they lay awake in their bunks,
cloaked in semidarkness, and they talked about
music. No matter where their conversation might
wander, it always returned to music.

"We weren't together today," said Emilio. "What
kind of musicians are we when we can't even keep
to the same tempo?"

"The drum is supposed to set the tempo. You just
don't listen to me," said Shlomo. "You're supposed
to follow *my* beat."

"How can we, with that French horn blasting in our ears?"

"So now it's *my* fault you can't stay together?" said Carlo.

"No one can hear anything except your damn horn. We're all deaf by the end of the day."

"I play the notes exactly as they're written. Don't blame me if it's *forte, forte, forte.* If you can't deal with it, then stuff rags in your ears!"

And so the nighttime conversations always went, always about music, never about what they'd seen and heard in the courtyard that day. Never about the trucks or their cargo or the foul smoke that rose from the chimney. Never about the real reason they were marched out every day with their instruments and music stands. One must not think about those things. No, better to block out those thoughts and fret instead about their ragged tempo in the second movement, and why did Vittorio always come in before the beat, and why must they play that tiresome "Blue Danube" again and again? The same complaints one might hear in symphony halls and jazz clubs everywhere. Death might be waiting for them in the wings, but they were still musicians. That was what sustained them; it was all they had to keep the terrors at bay.

But late in the night, when each man was alone with his thoughts, fear always crept in. How could it not, when a fresh set of screams erupted in Cell No. 1? Quick, clap your hands over your ears. Pull the blanket over your head and think about something else, anything else.

Laura. Waiting for me.

That was what Lorenzo always returned to: Laura, his light in the darkness. A sudden, vivid image of her bloomed in his head: Laura sitting by the window, her head bent over her cello, the sunlight gilding her hair. Her bow glides across the strings. The notes make the air hum and dust motes tremble like stars around her head. She plays a waltz, swaying to the rhythm, the cello pressed like a lover to her breast. What was that melody? He could almost, but not quite discern it. A minor key. Grace notes. An arpeggio soars in a heartbreaking crescendo. He struggled to hear it, but the music came to him in fractured bits and pieces, pierced through by screams.

He shuddered awake, the last tendrils of the dream still wrapped around him like loving arms. He heard the morning rumble of trucks and the thud of boots marching in the courtyard. Another dawn.

The music. What was that waltz Laura was playing in his dream? Suddenly desperate to write it down before he lost it forever, he reached under the mattress for the pencil and manuscript paper. There was barely enough light in the cell for him to see the notes he jotted onto the printed staves. He wrote quickly to get it all on paper before the melody faded. A waltz in E minor. An arpeggio up to G. He sketched out the first sixteen bars and gave a sigh of relief.

Yes, this was the basic melody, the underlying skeleton upon which the flesh of the waltz was built. But there was more to the music, much more. He wrote faster and faster until his pencil flew across the paper. The melody accelerated, notes scrambling upon notes, until the staves were dense with pencil marks. He flipped the page to its blank side and he could still hear the music playing, note after note, measure after measure. He wrote so frantically that his hand cramped and his neck ached. He did not notice daylight brightening through the bars. He did not hear the creak of the bunk beds as his cellmates stirred awake. All he heard was the music, Laura's music, heartbreaking and thrilling. Four of the measures weren't quite right; he erased and corrected them. Now he had only two blank staves left. How did the waltz end?

He closed his eyes and once again pictured Laura. He saw her hair aglow in a halo of sunlight. Saw her bow hover in a moment of silence, before it suddenly bites into the strings in a fierce double stop. What was earlier a frantic melody has slowed to the ponderous chords of a funeral dirge. There is no dramatic flourish at the end, no dazzling final run. There are just three final notes, muted and mournful, which fade into silence.

He set down his pencil.

"Lorenzo?" said Carlo. "What are you writing? What is that music?"

Lorenzo looked up and saw the other musicians staring at him. "It's a waltz," he said. "For the dying."

Julia ❦

18

After the crowds and noise of San Marco, it is un-
nervingly quiet on the narrow street where Francesca takes me. Late at night, tourists seldom
venture into this remote corner of the Castello
neighborhood, and the sound of Francesca's key
grating in the door lock seems dangerously loud.
We step into a dark apartment and I stand in the
shadows, bewildered, as she swiftly moves around
the room, closing blinds, shutting off any view of
the street. Only when all the windows are covered
does she dare turn on one small lamp. I had assumed this was her residence, but when I look
around the room I see faded brocade and lace doi-
lies and a frilly lampshade. These are not the usual
decorative choices of a young woman.

"It is my grandmother's apartment," explains
Francesca. "She stays in Milan this week. We will
wait here until Salvatore comes."

"We should call the police." I reach into my
purse, which I've somehow managed to hold on to

during my panicked dash through Dorsoduro. As I pull out the cellphone, she grabs my wrist.

"We cannot call the police," she says quietly.

"My friend has been shot! Of course we have to call them!"

"We can't trust them." She takes my phone and leads me to the sofa. "Please, Mrs. Ansdell. Sit down."

I sink onto frayed cushions. Suddenly I can't stop shaking and I wrap my arms around myself. Only now that I'm in a safe place can I allow myself to fall apart. I can almost feel myself cracking, disintegrating. "I don't understand. I don't understand why he wants me dead."

"I think I can explain," says Francesca.

"You? But you don't even know my husband!"

She frowns at me. "Your husband?"

"He sent that man to find me. To kill me." I wipe tears from my face. "Oh God, this can't be happening."

"No, no, no. This has nothing to do with your husband." She grabs me by the shoulders. "Listen to me. Please, listen."

I look up at eyes so intense I can almost feel their laser heat. She sits in a chair facing me, and for a moment she's silent, considering her next words. With her lustrous black hair and arched eyebrows, she could be a face in a Renaissance portrait. A dark-eyed madonna with a secret to share.

"Yesterday afternoon, after you left that piece of music with me, I made a number of phone calls," she says. "First, to a journalist I know. He verified that Mr. Padrone was indeed murdered during what appeared to be a robbery of his antiques shop. Then I called a contact in Rome, a woman who works with Europol, the law enforcement agency for the European Union. Just an hour ago, she called me back with very disturbing information. She said that although Mr. Padrone was killed during an apparent robbery, it was a very strange robbery. Money and jewelry in the shop were left untouched. All they found disturbed were a few shelves containing old books and music, but no one knows if anything was taken. Then she told me the most alarming detail of all: how Mr. Padrone was killed. Two bullets, to the back of his head."

I stare at her. "That sounds like an execution."

Francesca gives a grim nod. "These are the same people who want you dead." It is such a matter-of-fact statement, said in the same calm voice you might say, *and that's why the sky is blue*.

I shake my head. "No, that can't be right. Why would anyone want me dead?"

"The waltz. They now know you bought it from that shop. They know you're asking about the composer and where the music came from. That's why Mr. Padrone was killed, because he tried to find the answers for you. He spoke to the wrong people and asked some dangerous questions."

Incendio. It always comes back to the waltz.

"Do you know the answer?" I ask softly. "Where *does* the music come from?"

Francesca takes a deep breath, as if what she's about to tell me is a long and difficult tale. "I believe *Incendio* was indeed composed by Lorenzo Todesco, who was born and lived on Calle del

Forno until his arrest by the SS. He and his family—his parents, his sister and brother, were among the two hundred forty-six Jews who were deported from Venice. Of the entire Todesco family, only Marco returned alive. Marco died about ten years ago, but we have the transcript of an interview with him in our files at the museum. He described the night the family was arrested, their deportation, and the train that brought them to a death camp in Poland. He said his brother was separated from them in Trieste, after the guards identified Lorenzo as a musician."

"He was singled out because of *that*?"

"Lorenzo was among several musicians who were selected to remain in Risiera di San Sabba, also designated Stalag 339. Originally it was used as a transit camp and detention center for Italian prisoners. But as more and more prisoners passed through Trieste, the system became overwhelmed, and San Sabba's purpose changed. In 1944, the Germans constructed a highly efficient disposal system within the compound, to deal with all the executed prisoners."

"Disposal system," I murmur. "You mean . . ."

"A crematorium. It was designed by Erwin Lambert himself, the architect of gas chambers in Polish death camps. Thousands of political prisoners, partisans, and Jews were executed at San Sabba. Some died from torture. Some were shot or gassed or killed with a blow to the head from a club." She adds, quietly: "The dead were the fortunate ones."

"Why do you say that?"

"Because after execution, the next stop was the

crematorium. If by chance you survived the bullets or the club to the head or the poison gas, it meant you were fed to the ovens while still alive." Francesca pauses, and the silence magnifies the impact of her next statement. "The screams of those being burned alive could be heard throughout the compound."

Horror has rendered me speechless. I don't want to hear what comes next. I sit frozen, staring into Francesca's eyes.

"The shrieks were said to be so disturbing, even the Nazi commandant could not abide them. To mask that sound, as well as the sound of firing squads, he ordered music to be played in the courtyard. He appointed an Italian SS officer, a Colonel Collotti, for the task. In many ways it was a logical choice. Collotti considered himself a cultured man. He was an ardent fan of the symphony and was a collector of obscure music. He assembled an orchestra composed of prisoners. He personally selected his musicians and chose the music to be played. Among the pieces regularly performed was a waltz, which had been composed by one of the prisoner musicians. After the war, during testimony at trial, one of the prison guards described that waltz as haunting and beautiful, with a diabolical finish. It was Collotti's favorite piece and he ordered it played again and again. For thousands of condemned prisoners who were marched to their executions, that waltz was the last music they heard."

"*Incendio*. The fire."

Francesca nods. "The fire of the crematorium."

I am shaking again, feeling so cold that my teeth chatter. Francesca disappears into the kitchen and comes out moments later with a cup of steaming tea. Even as I sip, I cannot shake off the chill. Now I know the waltz truly is haunted, by the thousands of terrified souls who heard it playing as they drew their last breaths. It is a waltz to die by.

It takes me a long time to draw up the courage for my next question. "Do you know what happened to Lorenzo Todesco?"

She nods. "Before they fled, the Germans blew up the crematorium. But they left behind meticulously kept records, so we know the names of the prisoners and their ultimate fates. In October of 1944, Lorenzo Todesco and his fellow musicians were marched to their own executions. Their bodies were fed to the oven."

I sit in silence, my head bowed in sorrow for Lorenzo, for those who died with him, for everyone who perished in the inferno of war. I mourn the music that was never written, the masterpieces that will never be heard. The only thing he left us is a single waltz, composed by a man who wrote the soundtrack to his own doom.

"So now we know the history of *Incendio*," I say softly.

"Not entirely. There is still one burning question. How did the music find its way from the death camp of San Sabba to Mr. Padrone's antiques shop?"

I look up at her. "Is that important?"

Francesca rocks forward, her eyes fever-bright. "Think about it. We know it didn't come from the

musicians, who all perished. So it must have been
salvaged by one of the guards or SS officers who
fled before they could be arrested." She tilts her
head, watching me. Waiting for me to make the
connections.

"It came from the estate of Giovanni Capobianco."

"Yes! And that name *Capobianco* is like a flashing red light. I asked my friend at Europol to dig
into the background of this deceased Mr. Capobianco. We know he arrived in the village of Casperia around 1946. He lived there until his death
fourteen years ago, at the age of ninety-four. No
one in town knew where he came from, and they
said he was a very private man. He and his wife,
who died years before him, had three sons. When
he passed away, the estate agent working for the
family sold off most of his belongings, including a
large number of music books and fine instruments.
It was known that Mr. Capobianco was an ardent
fan of the symphony. He was also a man about
whom we can find absolutely no information. Until
his sudden and rather mysterious appearance in
1946."

A collector of music. A fan of the symphony. I
stare at Francesca. "He was Colonel Collotti."

"I'm sure of it. Collotti, like the other SS officers,
fled San Sabba before the Allies arrived. Authorities searched for him, but he was never found,
never brought to justice. I think he became Mr.
Capobianco, lived to a peaceful old age, and went
to his grave with his secret intact." Her voice is

tight with anger. "And they will do everything they can to keep it that way."

"He's dead now. Why would his secret matter to anyone?"

"Oh, that secret matters very much to certain people. People in power. This is why Salvatore and I came to find you tonight. To warn you." She pulls an Italian newspaper from her purse and spreads it out on the coffee table. On the front page is a photo of a handsome man in his forties, shaking hands amid an admiring crowd. "This is one of the fastest-rising stars in Italian politics and he's expected to win the next parliamentary election. Many predict he will be our next prime minister. For years his family has groomed him for this position. They've pinned their hopes on him, and what he can do for their business interests. His name is Massimo Capobianco." She looks at my startled face. "Who now appears to be the grandson of a war criminal."

"But *he* didn't commit war crimes. His grandfather did."

"And did he know about his grandfather's past? Did his family hide it all these years? That is the true scandal: how the Capobianco family, perhaps even Massimo himself, *reacted* to the threat of exposure." She looks straight at me. "Consider Mr. Padrone's murder. Perhaps it was to keep the family's secret from ever being revealed."

Which makes me responsible for the old man's death. At my request, Mr. Padrone asked the Capobianco family how their dead grandfather came to own an obscure waltz by a composer from Venice.

How long did it take them to discover that L. Todesco was a Jew who'd perished at Risiera di San Sabba? That the mere existence of that music proved Mr. Capobianco had *also* been at that same death camp?

"I believe this is why you were attacked," says Francesca. "Somehow, the Capobianco family learned you are here, in Venice."

"Because I told them," I whisper.

"What?"

"I asked the hotel clerk to call the Capobianco family about the music. I left my name and contact information."

Francesca gives a troubled shake of the head. "Now it's more important than ever to keep you out of sight."

"But *you* have the music now. You have the original. There's no reason for them to come after me."

"Yes, there is. You are a witness. You can testify that you bought the document from Mr. Padrone. And Anna Maria's letter clearly states that Mr. Padrone acquired it from the Capobiancos. You are the vital link in the chain of evidence leading directly to their family." She leans in, her expression fierce. "I'm a Jew, Mrs. Ansdell. So is Salvatore. There are very few of us left in this city, but the ghosts are still here, all around us. Now we can put this one to rest. The ghost of Lorenzo Todesco."

Someone knocks on the door, and I snap taut in alarm. "What do we do?" I whisper.

"Get down. Stay low." Francesca turns off the lamp, plunging us into darkness. I drop to the floor and feel my heart hammering against the carpet as

Francesca quietly makes her way through the shadows. At the door she calls out in Italian. A man answers.

With a sigh of relief, she opens the door to let him in, and when the light comes on again, I see Salvatore. I also see, from his tense face, that I'm not the only one who's frightened. He speaks rapidly to Francesca, who translates.

"He says three people were shot outside your hotel," she tells me. "One man is dead, but your friend was still alive when they took her to the hospital."

I think of the two unfortunate men who'd stepped out of the hotel, interrupting what would have been my murder. And I think of Gerda, who may now be struggling for her life.

"I have to call the hospital."

Once again, she stops me. "It's not safe."

"I need to know if my friend is all right!"

"You *need* to stay hidden. If something happens to you, if you can't testify against them, our chain of proof breaks. That's why Salvatore proposes this option."

He reaches into the backpack that he's carried into the apartment. I'm hoping he has a gun in there, something to defend us. Instead he pulls out a camera and tripod and proceeds to set it up in front of me.

"We must record your statement on video," says Francesca. "Should something happen to you, at least we'll have . . ." She stops, realizing how cold-blooded she must sound.

I finish her sentence. "You'll have my testimony on camera."

"Please understand, you are a threat to a very powerful family. We need to prepare for every possibility."

"Yes. I do understand." I understand that here, at last, is a way to fight back. For too long I've been flailing helplessly against an unknown threat. Now I know who my enemy is, and I have the power to bring him down. It's a job that only I can do. That thought steadies me, and I take a deep breath. I sit up and look straight at the camera. "What should I say?"

"Why don't you start with your name and address? Who you are and how you came to buy the music from Mr. Padrone. Tell us about what his granddaughter wrote to you. Tell us everything."

Everything. I think about what they have not yet heard. How the music transformed my daughter, and now I'm afraid of her. About the psychiatrist who wants to lock me in a mental ward. About my husband, who thinks I'm insane for believing *Incendio* has brought evil into our family. No, these are things I won't tell them, even though these things are all true. Evil *does* cling to *Incendio,* an evil that invaded my home and stole my daughter from me. The only way I can fight it is by exposing its terrible history.

"I'm ready," I tell them.

Salvatore presses the record button. A single red light glows on the camera like a malevolent eye.

I speak calmly and clearly. "My name is Julia Ansdell. I am thirty-three years old and married to

Robert Ansdell. We live at 4122 Heath Road in Brookline, Massachusetts. On June twenty-first, I visited the antiques shop of a Mr. Padrone in Rome, where I purchased a handwritten composition called *Incendio,* by a composer named L. Todesco. . . ."

The camera's red eye starts to blink. As Salvatore hunts for a fresh battery, I keep talking. About my search for Lorenzo's identity. About how I learned of Mr. Padrone's death. About . . .

19

I hear the sound of my own labored breathing. Smell the scent of my own fear. I am running down a dark alley. I don't remember what happened or how I escaped the apartment; I don't remember what became of Francesca or Salvatore. The last thing I do remember is sitting in front of the camera and the low-battery light blinking red. Something terrible has certainly happened, something that's left my arm cut and bleeding and my head pounding. I'm lost in a neighborhood I do not recognize.

And I am being followed.

From somewhere ahead comes the sound of thumping music, a primitive, driving beat. Where there's music, there are crowds where I can hide. I round a corner and see a busy nightclub and people standing outside at cocktail tables. But even here I am too easy to spot. My pursuer could simply pump a bullet into my back and melt away without ever being seen.

I push through the partygoers, hear a woman's

outraged yelp as I knock over her drink. Glass shatters on the cobblestones, but I keep running. I head across a busy piazza, pause to glance back. There are so many people that at first I can't be sure I'm still being followed. Then I spot a dark-haired man striding toward me with robotlike purpose. He is unstoppable.

I sprint around another corner and spot a sign for Piazza San Marco, pointing left. San Marco is ground zero for revelers in Venice, the place where you can find crowds even late into the night. It's exactly where he'll expect me to flee.

I turn right and duck into the cover of a doorway. I hear footsteps pound around the corner and then fade away. Toward San Marco.

I peek out of the doorway and see that the alley is now deserted.

Twenty minutes later, I find an unlocked gate and I slip into a private garden, where the shadows are fragrant with the scent of roses and thyme. The glow spilling out the upstairs windows is bright enough for me to see the bloodstains on my blouse. My left arm is crisscrossed with lacerations. From flying glass? An explosion? I don't remember.

I want to return to the apartment and see if Francesca and Salvatore are alive, and to retrieve my purse, but I know it's not safe to go back. Nor do I dare return to the hotel where Gerda was shot. I have no luggage, no purse, no credit cards, no cellphone. Frantically I search my pockets for cash, but all I find is a few loose coins and a single fifty-euro note.

It will have to be enough.

*   *   *

It takes me an hour to creep through alleys and dart across bridges before I finally make it to Venice's Santa Lucia train station. I don't dare go into the station itself, because it's the obvious place Capobianco's people would expect me to go. Instead I slip into one of the many Internet cafés and use some of my precious cash to buy an hour of computer time. It's past midnight, but the place is filled with backpacker types clacking away on keyboards. I settle in front of a computer far from the window, sign on to my email account, and search the Europol website for contact information. I don't see any way to directly email their investigative branch, so I address my message to their media office.

> My name is Julia Ansdell. I have vital information about the murder of Stefano Padrone, who was shot to death in Rome a few weeks ago. . . .

I write every detail I can remember about *Incendio* and Lorenzo Todesco and the Capobianco family. I tell them that my friend Gerda was shot outside our hotel, and Francesca and Salvatore may be dead. Will Europol dismiss me as a crazy conspiracy theorist? Or will they realize I am truly in danger and need their immediate help?

By the time I've finished typing, forty-five minutes have passed, and I'm exhilarated but drained. There is nothing more I can do but press Send and hope for the best. I send copies as well to the Jewish Museum in Venice, to Aunt Val, and to Rob. If I turn up murdered, at least they will know why.

The message whooshes into the ether.

I still have fifteen minutes left of computer time, so I open my inbox. I find five emails from Rob, the last one sent only two hours ago.

> I'm worried sick about you. Gerda doesn't answer her phone, so please let me know you're okay. A call, a text, anything. Whatever problems we've had, I promise we can fix them. I love you. I will never give up on you.

I stare at his words, wanting desperately to believe him.

The countdown starts to blink on the computer. I have only three minutes of Internet time remaining.

I begin to type.

> I'm scared and I need you. Do you remember the day I told you I was pregnant? That's where I'll be. The same time, the same place. Don't tell anyone.

I press Send.

My time on the computer is down to its last thirty seconds when a new email suddenly pops into my inbox. It's from Rob, and it's only four words long.

> Already on my way.

The city of Venice is the perfect place to hide. Honeycombed with countless narrow streets,

thronged with visitors from around the world, it is
easy to be lost among the crowd. At dawn, as the
streets start to come alive again, I emerge from the
cover of the archway where I've sheltered through
the night. I find a market where I buy bread, fruit,
cheese, and a desperately needed cup of coffee. Just
like that, the rest of my fifty euros is gone and now
I'm flat broke. There's nothing I can do but stay
alive and hidden until Rob comes for me. I know
he *will* come, if only because he doesn't like unfin-
ished equations.

I spend the day trying to stay out of sight. I avoid
the train station and vaporetti landings, where my
pursuers are no doubt searching for me. Instead I
find sanctuary inside a modest-looking church at
the outer edge of Cannaregio. St. Alvise's façade is
plain and unpretentious, but its jewel-like interior
is rich with frescoes and paintings. It's also cool
and quiet, and only two women sit inside, their
heads bowed in contemplation. I settle onto a pew
and wait out the hours. I want desperately to find
out if Gerda is alive, but I'm afraid to show my
face at the hospital. I'm also afraid of going anywhere near the Jewish Museum, and Francesca
told me that not even the police can be trusted. I
am on my own.

The two women leave and a few other worship-
pers trickle in to pray and light candles. None of
the visitors are tourists; St. Alvise is too far off the
beaten track.

At 4 P.M. I finally emerge from my sanctuary. I
step out into afternoon sunshine that's so glaring, I
feel painfully exposed as I make my way toward

the Rialto Bridge. The crowds grow thicker. The heat is so oppressive that everyone seems to move in slow motion, as if wading through syrup. It was four years ago, on an afternoon just this hot, that I broke the news to Rob that at long last, we were going to have a baby. We'd been walking for hours, and halfway across the Rialto Bridge, I hit such a wall of exhaustion that I had to stop and catch my breath.

Are you sick?

No. But I think I'm pregnant.

It was one of those moments of such pure happiness that I remember every detail. The briny smell from the canal. The taste of his lips on mine. It's a memory that only one other person shares with me. He alone knows where I'll be waiting.

I join the tourists streaming onto the bridge and am quickly swallowed up by the amoeba-like crowd. Halfway across, I stop at a vendor's cart where jewelry made of Venetian glass is displayed and I examine the array of necklaces and earrings. I linger so long that the vendor thinks he's about to make a sale, even though I keep telling him I'm only looking. We're joined by his female assistant, who noisily offers me discounts, her voice so strident that people look at us. As I retreat, she calls out even louder, annoyed that her customer is slipping away.

"Julia," a voice says behind me.

I turn and there he is, unshaven and rumpled. He looks like he has not slept in days, and when he throws his arms around me, I can smell his fear, ripe as sweat.

"It's okay," he murmurs. "I'll take you home now and everything will be fine."

"I can't just get on a plane, Rob. It's not safe."

"Of course it is."

"You don't know everything that's happened. They're trying to kill me!"

"And that's why these men are here to protect you. They'll keep you safe. You just have to trust them."

Them?

Only then do I spot the two men moving in. There's nowhere for me to run, no possible escape. Rob's arms close around me, trapping me against him.

"Julia, darling, I'm doing this for you," he says. "For us."

I battle to get free, but even as I claw and flail at him, Rob holds on tight, squeezing so hard I think he will crush the life out of me. I see a sudden flash, bright as a thousand exploding suns. And then, nothing.

20

Through the haze blurring my vision, I can just make out the image of a woman. She wears a flowing blue robe and she stares upward, her clasped hands reaching toward heaven. It's a portrait of some saint, although I do not know her name. The painting on the wall is the only color I see in this room where the walls are white, the sheets are white, the window blinds are white. Through the closed door, I hear voices speaking Italian and the rattle of a cart rolling down the hall.

I don't remember how I came to be here, but I know exactly where I am. A hospital. Dextrose and water drips from an IV bag into the intravenous line that snakes its way into my left hand. Nearby is a bedside tray with a pitcher of water, and around my wrist is a plastic ID band with my name and birth date. It does not say which ward I'm in, but I assume I'm in some Italian loony bin where I can't even communicate with my doctors. I wonder if there's an extradition agreement for mental patients, the way there is for criminals. Will Italy ship me home, or am I doomed to forever stare at that blue-robed saint on the wall?

I hear footsteps in the hallway and I snap straight up in bed as the door opens and Rob walks in. But he's not the one I stare at; my gaze is fixed on the woman beside him.

"How are you feeling?" she asks.

I shake my head in bewilderment. "You're here. You're alive."

Francesca nods. "Salvatore and I were so worried about you! After you ran from the apartment, we searched everywhere. All night."

"I ran? But I thought . . ."

"You don't remember?"

My skull is pounding and I massage my temples as I struggle to retrieve any memories from last night. Images flit by. A dark alley. A garden gate. Then I remember my bloodstained blouse and I look down at the bandaged cuts on my arm. "How did I get these? Was there an explosion?" •

She shakes her head. "There was no explosion."

Rob sits down on the bed and takes my hand. "Julia, there's something you need to see. It will explain the cuts on your arm. It will explain everything that's happened to you these past few weeks." He looks at Francesca. "Show her the video."

"What video?" I ask.

"The one we recorded last night, in my grandmother's apartment." Francesca reaches into the computer bag she's carried into the room and pulls out a laptop. She turns the screen toward me and starts the video. I see my own face, hear my own voice.

"*My name is Julia Ansdell. I am thirty-three years old and married to Robert Ansdell. We live at 4122 Heath Road in Brookline, Massachusetts. . . .*"

On-screen I look nervous and disheveled, and I keep glancing sideways at the two people who are off camera. But I do not falter as I explain the story of *Incendio*. How I bought it from Mr. Padrone. How I came to Venice in search of answers. How Gerda and I were attacked outside our hotel.

"*I swear that everything I've just said is the truth. If anything happens to me, at least you'll know . . .*"

My face abruptly goes blank. A moment passes in silence.

On the recording, an off-camera Francesca says: "Julia, what's wrong?" She comes into view and taps my shoulder, then gives me a gentle shake. I don't respond. She frowns and says something in Italian to Salvatore.

The camera is still recording as I rise like a robot and walk out of view. Francesca and Salvatore call out to me. There are loud bangs and the sound of shattering glass, and then Francesca's alarmed shout: "Where are you going? Come back!"

Francesca freezes the video, and all I see on-screen is a view of the empty chair where I had earlier been seated. "You broke a window and you ran away from us," she says. "We called our museum colleagues to help search, but we couldn't find you. So we used your cellphone, the one in your purse, to call your husband. It turned out he was already at the airport in Boston, waiting to board a flight to Venice."

"I don't understand," I whisper, staring at the laptop screen. "Why did I do that? What's wrong with me?"

"Sweetheart, I think we know the answer," says Rob. "When you were admitted to the hospital a few hours ago, you were unresponsive, as if you were in a catatonic state. The doctors did an emergency brain scan. That's when they understood the problem. They're confident it's benign and they can remove it, but you'll need surgery."

"Surgery? For what?"

He squeezes my hand and says, quietly: "You have a brain tumor pressing on your temporal lobe. It explains your headaches, your memory lapses. It could explain everything that's happened these past few weeks. Do you remember what Lily's neurologist told us about temporal lobe seizures? He said they can look like highly complex behaviors. People can walk, talk, even drive a car during a seizure. *You* were the one who killed Juniper. *You* stabbed yourself with broken glass. You just don't remember doing it. And when you woke up, you thought you heard Lily repeat the words *hurt Mommy, hurt Mommy*. But that's not what she was saying. I think she was really saying: *Mommy hurt. Mommy hurt*. She was afraid for you. Trying to comfort you."

My throat closes over and suddenly I am sobbing with relief. My daughter loves me. My daughter has always loved me.

"Everything you've been through," says Rob, "can be explained by the seizures. By the tumor."

"Not everything," says Francesca. "There is still the matter of *Incendio*, and where it comes from."

I shake my head. "Oh God, I'm so confused I don't know anymore what's real and what's imagined."

"You didn't imagine the man who tried to kill you. The man who shot your friend."

I look at Rob. "Gerda—"

"She'll be fine. She made it through surgery and she's recovering," he says.

"So that part was real? The shooting?"

"As real as the bodyguards who are now stationed outside your door," says Francesca. "Europol is investigating, and if what we suspect about the Capobianco family is true . . ." She smiles. "You've brought down the man who could have been our next prime minister. Congratulations. My colleagues at the museum think you are a hero."

It's a victory I hardly feel like celebrating, because I'm thinking about a far more intimate enemy, the tumor that is now incubating inside my brain. An enemy that so skewed my reality, it made me fear the people I love most. I think of how often I've massaged my aching temples, trying to soothe what was growing and swelling inside. An enemy that can yet defeat me.

But I'm no longer alone in this battle because Rob stands beside me. He has always been beside me, even when I did not know it.

Francesca packs up her laptop. "Now then, I

have work to do. Statements to prepare, documents to file. We are going to do a thorough search of the archives for everything we have about the Todesco family." She smiles at me. "And you have a job as well."

"Do I?"

"You need to get better, Mrs. Ansdell. We're counting on it. You're the one who started us down this road. You must be the one to tell the story of *Incendio*."

21

Eight Years Later

On Calle del Forno, a new plaque has been mounted on No. 11, where Lorenzo and his family once lived. It bears a simple inscription in Italian: "Here lived composer and violinist Lorenzo Todesco, who perished in the death camp at Risiera di San Sabba, October 1944." It says nothing about *Incendio* or Lorenzo's family or the circumstances of his final months at San Sabba, but there's no need to. Tonight, the new documentary about his life will be shown to the public for the first time. Soon everyone in Venice will know his story.

They'll know my story as well, because I'm the one who found *Incendio,* and tonight, at the film's Venice premiere, my quartet will perform the music. Though Lorenzo's body was long ago consumed by the flames of San Sabba's crematorium, his composition is still powerful enough to change lives. It brought down the man who might have been prime minister. It alerted me to the meningioma that was once growing in my brain. And this evening, it has brought an international crowd into the university auditorium at Ca' Foscari, to watch the film *Incendio* and to hear the waltz that inspired it.

Backstage, I feel eerily calm despite the noisy chatter of the audience, which we can hear through the closed curtain. There's a full house tonight, and Gerda's so excited she keeps drumming her fingers against the back of her violin. I can hear our cellist standing behind me, nervously fussing with her black taffeta skirt.

The curtain rises and we walk out onto the stage and take our seats.

In the blinding glare of the stage lights I cannot see the audience, but I know that Rob and Lily and Val are watching from the middle section, the third row, as I lift my bow to my violin. No longer am I afraid of this music, which once ignited electrical storms inside my brain. Yes, it comes with a haunting history, and death has followed it from one century to the next, but it bears no curse, carries no misfortune. In the end, it is just a waltz, a long-delayed echo of the same notes that Lorenzo Todesco once played, and it is beautiful. I wonder if Lorenzo's spirit can hear us play it. Do the notes that fly from our strings somehow cross dimensions and find him wherever he now dwells? If he can hear us, then he knows he's not forgotten. And that, in the end, is what we all hope for: to never be forgotten.

We come to the final measure. The last note is Gerda's, and it is high and sweet and heartbreaking, like a kiss blown to heaven. The audience sits stunned and silent, as if no one wants to disturb the sanctity of that moment. When the applause comes, it is thunderous. *Do you hear that applause, Lorenzo? It comes seventy years too late, but it's all for you.*

Afterward, in the greenroom, the four of us are delighted to find a bottle of prosecco chilling in an ice bucket. Gerda pops the cork and we toast our performance with the musical clink of champagne flutes.

"We've never sounded better!" Gerda says. "Next stop, the London premiere!"

Another clink of flutes, another round of self-congratulatory laughter. On a night when we honor the life of Lorenzo Todesco, it seems wrong to be so lighthearted, and this is only the start of the night's festivities. Even as we pack up our instruments, the filmmaker's party is already under way in the courtyard outside, an evening of dining and dancing under the stars. Gerda and the others are eager to join the celebration and they lead the way out of the greenroom and down the hallway toward the auditorium exit.

I'm about to follow them out of the building when a voice calls out behind me: "Mrs. Ansdell?"

Turning, I see a woman in her sixties, with silver-streaked black hair and dark, serious eyes. "I'm Julia Ansdell," I answer. "How can I help you?"

"I read your interview in the newspaper yesterday," the woman says. "The article about *Incendio* and the Todesco family."

"Yes?"

"There is a part of the story that was not mentioned in the article. The Todescos are all dead now, so there's no way you could have heard about it. But I think you might like to know."

I frown at her. "Is this about Lorenzo?"

"In a way. But it's really about a young woman named Laura Balboni. And what happened to her."

My visitor's name is Clementina. She was born in Venice, and she teaches English in a local high school, which is why she speaks with such fluency. Gerda and the others have already left the auditorium to join the party, so Clementina and I are alone in the greenroom, where we sit on a lumpy sofa with faded upholstery. Clementina tells me she learned this story from her late aunt, who worked as housekeeper for a Professor Balboni, a distinguished musicologist who taught at Ca' Foscari. The professor was a widower with one child, a daughter named Laura.

"My aunt Alda told me this girl was beautiful and talented. And fearless," says Clementina. "So fearless that, as a very small child, Laura once climbed onto a chair to see what was bubbling on the stove. The pot tipped and she burned her arms so badly that she was left with terrible scars. Yet she never tried to hide those scars. She bravely revealed them to the world."

"You said your story has a connection with Lorenzo," I remind her.

"Yes, and this is where our two stories merge," says Clementina. "With Laura and Lorenzo. You see, they were in love."

I lean forward, excited by this new revelation. Up till now, I'd focused only on Lorenzo's tragic end. Here was a detail not about his death, but about his life. "I didn't know about Laura Balboni. How did she and Lorenzo meet?"

Clementina smiles. "It was because of music, Mrs. Ansdell. It all started with music."

The music of a violin and a cello, blended in perfect harmony, she explains. Every Wednesday, Laura and Lorenzo would meet in Laura's home in Dorsoduro, to practice the duet that they would perform for a prestigious competition at Ca' Foscari. I picture the two of them, dark-eyed Lorenzo and golden-haired Laura, alone together for hour after hour, struggling to master their piece. How many sessions did it take for them to finally look up from their music stands and focus only on each other?

Did they realize, as they were falling in love, that the world was collapsing around them?

"When the SS took control of Venice, Laura tried to save him," Clementina tells me. "She and her father did everything they could to help the Todesco family, at great risk to themselves. The Balbonis were Catholic, but what difference does that make when it comes to matters of the heart? Certainly it did not matter to Laura, who loved him. But in the end, there was nothing she could do to save Lorenzo or his family. She was there, the day they were deported. She watched them marched to the train station. And that was the last time she ever saw him."

"What became of her?"

"My aunt said the poor girl never gave up hope

that Lorenzo would come back to her. She read and reread the letter he sent her from the train. He wrote that his family was fine, and he was certain the labor camp would not be so terrible. He promised to come home to her, if only she would wait for him. And for months, she *did* wait, but there was no more news."

"So she had no idea what happened to him?"

"How could she possibly know? That letter from the train was enough to give her hope, because she believed he was bound for nothing worse than a labor camp. That was the reason why detainees aboard the train were encouraged to write letters and assure their friends that all was well. Here at home, no one suspected where the train was taking them. No one imagined they were bound for Poland, where they'd all be . . ." Clementina's voice fades.

"Did Laura ever find out what happened to him?"

"No."

"But she *did* wait? When the war ended, she *did* search for him?"

Clementina gives a sad shake of the head.

I sink back on the sofa, disappointed. I had expected this to be a story of devotion, of lovers who remained steadfast even after war had ripped them apart. But Laura Balboni did not keep her promise to wait for Lorenzo. This is not, after all, the tale of enduring love that I had wanted to hear.

"Well, you mentioned that she was beautiful," I say. "I'm sure there was another man for her."

"There was no one else. Not for Laura."

"So she never married?"

The woman looks past me, her eyes unfocused, as though I'm not even in the room and she's talking to someone I cannot see. "It happened in May 1944. Five months after the Todescos were deported," she says softly. "The world was at war and everywhere in Europe, there was death and tragedy. Yet it was a beautiful springtime, I'm told. The seasons don't care how many corpses lie rotting in the fields; the flowers will still bloom.

"My aunt Alda said that it was late in the night when the family appeared at Professor Balboni's door. A couple and their two young sons. They were Jews who'd been hiding for months in a neighbor's attic, but the SS was closing in, and they were desperate to flee to Switzerland. They'd heard that the professor was sympathetic, and could he shelter them for just one night? My aunt Alda warned him that it was too dangerous to let them stay. The SS was already aware of his political leanings, and they might raid the house. She knew it could bring disaster on them."

"Did he listen to your aunt?"

"No. Because Laura—brave, headstrong Laura—wouldn't allow the family to be turned away. She said, what if Lorenzo was standing on some stranger's doorstep at that very moment, also pleading for sanctuary? She couldn't bear the thought of him being turned away. She convinced her father to take in the family that night."

Dread has made my hands go cold.

"The next morning, my aunt Alda left to go to the market," continues Clementina. "When she returned, she found the SS raiding the house, kicking open doors, smashing furniture. The Jews who'd taken shelter with the Balbonis were arrested and later deported to a Polish death camp. And the Balbonis . . ." She pauses, as if she hasn't the heart to continue.

"What happened to them?"

Clementina takes a deep breath. "Professor Balboni and his daughter were dragged out of the house. There, by the canal, they were forced to kneel in the street as public examples of what happens when you dare to hide a Jew. They were executed on the spot."

I cannot speak. I cannot even breathe. I bow my head and wipe away tears for a young woman I have never met. On the spring day that Laura Balboni was executed, Lorenzo was still alive. He did not perish in San Sabba until that autumn, when the girl he loved had already been dead for months. Though he could not have known she was gone, did he somehow sense her passing? As her soul departed, did he hear her voice in his dreams, feel the whisper of her breath against his skin? When he marched to his own execution, did he take comfort in knowing that he was also marching toward Laura? She had promised to wait for him, and there she would be, ready to welcome him on the other side of death.

That's what I want to believe.

"Now you know the rest of the story," Clementina says. "Laura's story."

"And I knew nothing about her." I take a deep

breath. "Thank you. I would never have heard her name if you hadn't told me."

"I told you because it is important to remember more than just the victims. We must also remember the heroes, don't you think, Mrs. Ansdell?" She rises to her feet. "It was good to meet you."

"Mommy, *there* you are!" My eleven-year-old daughter comes running into the greenroom. Lily's hair has come loose from her braid, and riotous blond strands fly around her face. "Daddy's been looking all over for you. Why aren't you outside with us? They've started the party in the courtyard and everyone's dancing. You should hear what Gerda's playing. It's some crazy klezmer tune!"

I rise to my feet. "I'm coming now, darling."

"So this is your daughter," says Clementina.

"Her name's Lily."

They share a polite handshake and Clementina asks her: "Are you a musician like your mother?"

Lily beams. "I'd like to be."

"She already is," I say proudly. "Lily has a far better ear than I ever will, and she's only eleven years old. You should hear her play."

"Do you play the violin?"

"No," says Lily. "I play the cello."

"The cello," Clementina repeats softly, staring at my daughter. Although her lips are smiling, there is a sadness to the woman's eyes, as if she's gazing at the photograph of someone she once knew. Someone who has long since vanished from this earth. "I'm glad to meet you, Lily," she says. "Someday, I hope I *will* hear you play."

My daughter and I emerge from the building into

a velvety summer evening. Lily doesn't just walk, but half-dances beside me, a golden-haired sprite in sandals and flowery cotton who skips across the cobblestones. We cross the courtyard, past groups of university students laughing and chattering in Italian, past a stone fountain where water splashes its own sweet melody. Overhead pigeons swoop like white-winged angels in the dusk, and I smell the scent of roses and the sea.

Somewhere ahead of us a violin is playing klezmer music. It is a happy, raucous tune, and it makes me want to dance, to clap.

To live.

"You hear that, Mommy?" Lily tugs me forward. "Come on, you're going to miss the party!"

Laughing, I take my daughter's hand, and together, we join the music.

Historical Notes

It is hard to believe, walking in today's Campo Ghetto Nuovo, that this serene Venetian square was once a place of such tragedy. Memorial plaques mounted on the walls of the square tell the heartbreaking story of the nearly 250 Jews in Venice who were arrested and deported in 1943 and 1944. Only eight returned alive. During these terrible years, 20 percent of Italy's 47,000 Jews perished, most of them killed in death camps.

As staggering as these numbers are, they pale in comparison to what was happening to Jews elsewhere in occupied Europe. In Poland and Germany and the Baltic, 90 percent of the Jewish population was annihilated. In the Netherlands, 75 percent vanished into death camps, and in Belgium, 60 percent. Why did a greater percentage of Jews survive in Italy? What made Italy different?

That issue preoccupied me as I wandered the narrow streets of Cannaregio, the Venice neighborhood where many Jews once lived. Was there something unique in the Italian character that made Italians disregard, even actively resist, laws that they felt were unjust? As one who is drawn back to Italy again and again, who's fallen in love with its people, I *wanted* to believe that Italians are special. But I know all too well that every country has its dark side.

That question of "What made Italy different?" is addressed in two excellent books: Susan Zuccotti's *The Italians and the Holocaust,* and Renzo De Felice's *The Jews in Fascist Italy.* Both authors agree that for Jews, Italy *was* different in many ways from the rest of occupied Europe. Well assimilated and physically indistinguishable from their neighbors, Jews easily blended into the larger population. Before the war, they held high positions in government, academics, business, medicine, and law. Forty-four percent of their marriages were to non-Jews. In every way, they must have felt fully integrated in Italian society; even Benito Mussolini's mistress and biographer, the highly accomplished Margherita Sarfatti, was a Jew.

But security is too often an illusion, and throughout the 1930s Jews gradually realized that even in Italy, the ground beneath them was transforming into dangerous quicksand. At first the signs were merely worrisome: the appearance of several anti-Semitic editorials in a number of publications, followed by the dismissal of Jewish journalists from the newspaper *Il Popolo d'Italia.* By 1938, the campaign against them had accelerated, leading to a succession of ever more onerous laws. In September 1938, Jews were banned from teaching or enrolling in schools. In November 1938, intermarriage was forbidden and Jews were cast out of state employment. In June 1939, they were banned from skilled professions, putting doctors, lawyers, architects, and engineers out of work. They could not own radios or enter public buildings. They could not visit popular vacation spots. Music composed by Jews could not be broadcast on the radio.

As the laws grew progressively more outrageous, some chose to leave the country, but most remained. Even as the danger signs accumulated, they could not believe that what was happening in Germany and Poland would ever happen in Italy. Like the metaphorical frog being boiled alive in a slowly heating pot of water, most Italian Jews adapted to the harsh new realities and simply went on with their lives. For families like Lorenzo's, families who had lived in Italy for centuries, where else would they go?

In 1943, with the German occupation of northern and central Italy, these families found themselves trapped. As the German and Italian SS hunted them down, Jews scrambled to hide or escape. Some made it safely over the mountains to Switzerland. Some were taken in by nuns or priests and were sheltered in monasteries or convents. Some hid in the homes of sympathetic friends or neighbors.

But too many were arrested and deported like Lorenzo's family, sent by train to destinations north. Most believed they were headed to labor camps; few could have imagined their journeys would end in Polish crematoriums.

In Venice, disaster struck with such suddenness that they were surprised in their beds. In early December 1943, as air raid sirens wailed to drown out any cries, authorities rounded up close to a hundred Jews. Imprisoned temporarily in a school that had been transformed into a detention center, they went without food for days, until pitying neighbors tossed food through the windows. Half-starved, marched to the waiting train that would transport them out of the city, the detainees must still have believed they would survive, as many of them wrote reassuring letters home to their friends in Venice.

Their journey to Auschwitz would have brought them through the transit camp at Risiera di San Sabba, on the outskirts of Trieste. Originally built as a rice-husking factory, Risiera di San Sabba was converted into the only extermination camp on Italian soil. By the spring of 1944, it was furnished with its own crematorium, the final destination for thousands of executed political prisoners, Resistance fighters, and Jews. The noise of the executions, and sometimes the screams from the oven itself, were said to be so disturbing that music was played to drown out the sounds.

In this brutal historical landscape, it is easy to identify villains, from the politicians who campaigned for anti-Semitic laws, to the fascist police who willingly arrested and deported their fellow Italians, to the informants who betrayed their neighbors and colleagues. But it is just as easy to find heroes: Professor Giuseppe Jona, who, when ordered to turn over the names of his fellow Jews in Venice, instead destroyed the lists and committed suicide; the thousands of Resistance fighters, many of whom died at the hands of torturers in San Sabba; the sympathetic *carabinieri,* police officials who refused to round up local Jews and even assisted in their concealment; and the countless nuns, priests, and everyday Italians who fed, clothed, and sheltered strangers who were in desperate need.

Like the Balbonis, some of these unsung heroes paid for their deeds with their lives.

These are the people I wanted to honor in *Playing with Fire,* these ordinary men and women whose quiet acts of humanity and sacrifice give us all hope. Even in the darkest of times, there will always be a Laura to light the way.

For Further Reading

Susan Zuccotti, *The Italians and the Holocaust.* Lincoln: University of Nebraska Press, 1996.

Renzo De Felice, *The Jews in Fascist Italy.* New York: Enigma Books, 2001.

"The Holocaust in Italy." United States Holocaust Memorial Museum. ushmm.org/learn/mapping-initiatives/geographies-of-the-holocaust/the-holocaust-in-italy

"Risiera di San Sabba." Museum website: risierasansabba.it

Acknowledgments

The power of music to inspire and to change lives, even across the centuries, is at the heart of *Playing with Fire*. I'm grateful to all the people who brought the gift of music into my life: my parents, who knew I would someday thank them for all those long and tedious hours of practice on the piano and violin; my music teachers, who patiently endured all my sour notes; and my Maine jam session buddies, with whom I've shared many a raucous night trading tunes. Musicians are the warmest, most generous people in the world, and I feel blessed to be part of their circle. In particular I thank Janet Ciano, who lovingly inspired a whole generation of string players; Chuck Markowitz, who shares my love of just fooling around on fiddles; and Heidi Karod, for being the very first to play *Incendio*.

I'm grateful for the steadfast support from my literary agent, Meg Ruley, my editors Linda Marrow (Ballantine) and Sarah Adams (Transworld

UK), and a publishing team that spans both sides of The Pond: Libby McGuire, Sharon Propson, Gina Centrello, Kim Hovey, Larry Finlay, and Alison Barrow. You are all a joy to work with!

Most of all, I thank my husband, Jacob, who has stood beside me through every high and low of my career. It's a tough job being a writer's spouse, and nobody does it better.

Read on for an exciting peek at

Rizzoli & Isles:
Strange Girl

By Tess Gerritsen

Even monsters were mortal.

The woman lying on the other side of the window might appear to be as human as the other patients in the intensive care unit, but Dr. Maura Isles knew only too well that Amalthea Lank was indeed a monster. Beyond the cubicle window was the creature who'd stalked Maura's nightmares, who cast a shadow over Maura's past, and whose face foretold Maura's future.

Here is my mother.

"We'd heard Mrs. Lank had a daughter, but we didn't realize you were right down the road in Boston," said Dr. Wang. Was that a note of criticism in his voice? Disapproval that she'd neglected her filial duties?

"She's my biological mother, but I only met her a few years ago. I was an infant when she gave me up for adoption," Maura said.

"So you were acquainted."

"We aren't at all close. In fact, I haven't spoken

to her since . . ." Maura paused. *Since I swore I'd have nothing more to do with her.* "I came because I heard she was in the ICU."

"She was moved here two days ago, after she developed a fever. Also, her white blood cell count is quite low."

"How low?"

"The neutrophil count—that's a specific type of white blood cell—is five hundred. That's only a third of what it should be."

"I assume you've started empiric antibiotics?" She looked at him. "I'm sorry, should have mentioned that I'm a physician. I work for the medical examiner's office."

"Oh. I didn't realize." He cleared his throat and instantly shifted to the language they shared as doctors. "Yes, we started antibiotics, including anti-pseudomonal therapy. About five percent of patients on her chemotherapy regimen get febrile neutropenia."

"Which chemo regimen is she on?"

"Folforinex. It's a combination of four drugs including fluorouracil and leucovorin. According to a French study, Folforinex definitely prolongs of life for patients with metastatic pancreatic cancer, but they have to be closely monitored for fevers. Fortunately, the prison nurse did a good job of that in Framingham." He paused. "I hope you don't mind me asking this question . . ."

"Yes?"

He looked away, clearly uncomfortable with the painful subject he was about to broach. How much easier it was to discuss blood counts and antibiotic protocols and cold scientific data. "The medical record that Framingham sent us didn't mention the reason why she's in prison. All we were told is that Mrs. Lank is serving a life term with no chance of parole. The guard keeps her handcuffed to the bedrail, which seems pretty inhumane."

"That's just protocol for hospitalized prisoners."

"Your mother's dying of pancreatic cancer. Look how frail she is. She's certainly not going to jump up and escape. But the guard said Mrs. Lank is a lot more dangerous than she looks."

"She is," said Maura softly.

"Can I ask why she's in prison?"

"Homicides. Multiple."

He blinked in surprise. *"Her?"*

"Yes. Now you understand the reason for the handcuffs. And the twenty-four-hour guard." Maura glanced at the uniformed officer who sat nearby, listening to their conversation.

"Wow. That's got to be hard for you. Knowing that—"

"My mother's a murderer? Yes." *And you don't know the worst of it. You don't know about the other monsters in the family.*

Through the cubicle window, Maura saw Amalthea's eyes slowly open. One bony finger beckoned to her, a gesture as chilling as a command by Satan's claw. I should turn and leave now, she thought. Amalthea did not deserve any pity, any kindness. But as repulsed as she was, Maura shared a bond with this woman, a bond that went all the way down to their molecules. If only by DNA, Amalthea Lank *was* her mother.

The guard watched as Maura donned an isolation gown and mask. This would be no private visit; through the viewing window, he would be observing their every look, every gesture, and the gossip would surely make the rounds of this hospital. Dr. Maura Isles, the Boston medical examiner whose scalpel had laid bare countless cadavers, was the daughter of a serial killer. Death ran in the family. Amalthea stared up at Maura with eyes as black as chips of obsidian. Oxygen hissed softly through her nasal prongs, and on the monitor above the bed, a cardiac rhythm blipped across the screen. Proof that even soulless Amalthea possessed a heart.

"You came after all," whispered Amalthea. "And you swore you never would."

"You're sick. I thought I should visit while I still could."

"And because you need something from me."

Maura gave a disbelieving shake of the head. "I need something from *you*?"

"It's the way of the world. All sensible creatures seek their own advantage."

"That may be how it is for you. Not for me."

"Then why did you come?"

"Because you're dying. Because you asked me to come. I like to think that I, at least, have some sense of humanity."

"Which I don't have."

"Why do you suppose you're handcuffed to that bed?"

Amalthea grimaced and closed her eyes. Her mouth suddenly tightened in pain. "I suppose I deserve that," she whispered, sweat glistening on her upper lip. For a moment she lay perfectly still, as though any movement, even drawing a breath, was too excruciating to bear. The last time Maura had seen her, Amalthea's hair had been thick and generously streaked with silver. Now only a few wisps clung to her scalp, the last survivors of a brutal round of chemotherapy. The flesh of her temples had wasted away and the skin sagged like a collapsing tent over the bones of her face. Beneath that final veil, the skull waited to emerge.

"Do you need morphine?" Maura asked. "I'll call the nurse."

Amalthea slowly released a breath. "Not yet. I want to be awake. I want to talk to you."

"About what?"

"Who you are, Maura."

"I know who I am."

"Do you, really?" Amalthea's eyes opened and looked at her. "You are my daughter."

"I'm nothing like you."

"Because you were raised by the kindly Mr. and Mrs. Isles in San Francisco? Because you went to the best schools, had the best education? Because you work on the side of truth and justice?"

"Because I didn't slaughter two dozen women. Or was it more? Were there victims that didn't show up in the final tally?"

"That's in the past. I want to talk about what happens next."

"Why? You won't be here." It was a heartless thing to say, but Maura was not in the mood to be charitable. Suddenly she felt manipulated, lured here by a woman who knew exactly which strings to pull. For months, Amalthea had sent her letters. *I'm dying of cancer. I'm your only blood relative. This will be your last chance to say goodbye.*

Few words held more power than *last chance.* Let the opportunity pass, and what followed could be a lifetime of regret.

"Yes, I'll be dead," said Amalthea. "And you'll be left to wonder who your people are."

"My people?" Maura laughed. "As if we're some sort of tribe?"

"We are. We belong to a tribe that profits off the dead. Your father and I did. Your brother did. And isn't it ironic that you profit off them as well? Ask yourself, Maura, why did you choose your profession? Why aren't you a teacher or a banker? What makes you slice open the dead?"

"The science. I want to understand."

"Of course. The intellectual answer."

"Is there another?"

"The darkness. We both share it. The difference is, I'm not afraid of it, but you are. You deal with that fear by cutting it open with your scalpels, hoping to reveal its secrets. But that doesn't work, does it? It doesn't solve your primary problem."

"Which is?"

"That it's inside you. It's part of you."

Maura stared into those obsidian eyes and what she saw there made her throat suddenly go dry. *I see myself.* She backed away. "I'm done here. You asked me to come and I did. Don't send me any more letters, because I won't read them." She turned. "Goodbye, Amalthea."

"You're not the only one I write to, you know."

Maura paused, about to open the cubicle door.

"He asked me to tell you something. He said, 'They'll find another one, soon.'"

Another what?

Maura hovered on the verge of walking out, struggling not to be sucked back into the conversation. Don't respond, she thought. Don't let her trap you here.

It was her cell phone that saved her, its deep-throated buzz trembling in her pocket. Without a backward glance, she stepped out of the cubicle, pulled off her face mask, and fumbled under the isolation gown for the phone. "Dr. Isles," she answered.

"Got an early Christmas present for you," said Detective Jane Rizzoli, sounding far too breezy for the news she was about to share. "Twenty-six year old female, found dead in bed."

"Where are you?"

"Leather District. Loft apartment on Utica Street. I can't *wait* to hear what you think about this one."

"You said she was found in bed. Is this clearly a homicide?"

"Oh, yeah. But it's what happened to her *afterward* that's got Frost freaking out here." Jane paused and added grimly, "At least, we *hope* this happened after she was dead."

Through the cubicle window, Amalthea was watching the conversation, eyes sharp with interest. Of course she would be interested; Death was their family trade.

"How soon can you get here?" said Jane.

"I'm in Framingham at the moment. It might take me a while, depending on traffic."

"Framingham? What're you doing out there?"

It was not a subject Maura wanted to discuss, certainly not with Jane. "I'm leaving now," was all she said. She hung up and looked through the cubicle window at her dying mother. I'm done here, she thought. I never have to see you again.

Amalthea's lips slowly curved into a smile.

By the time Maura drove into Boston, darkness had fallen and the bone-chilling wind had swept most pedestrians off the streets. As she stepped out of her Lexus, that wind whipped the hem of her long black coat and pierced straight through the fabric of her woolen trousers. She walked as quickly as she dared on a sidewalk glazed with ice, past a sandwich shop and a shuttered travel office, and rounded the corner onto Utica Street, which was little more than an alley between red-brick warehouses. Once this had been a district of leather workers and wholesalers, but many of these nineteenth-century buildings had recently been converted to loft apartments. What had been an industrial district was slowly transforming into a trendy neighborhood of artists.

Maura stepped around construction rubbish that partially blocked the already narrow street, and spied blue cruiser lights flashing ahead, a grim homing beacon in the darkness. Two patrolmen were sitting inside the vehicle, their engine running to keep the heater on. They spied her approaching and a cruiser window rolled down.

"Hey, Dr. Isles, you missed the excitement. The ambulance just left." Though the officer looked familiar, she did not know his name, something that happened all too frequently.

"What happened?"

"Rizzoli was out here talking to some guy when he clutches his chest and doubles over. Probably a heart attack. Should've been here. They could've used a doctor."

"I'm not that kind of doctor." She turned to the building. "Rizzoli inside?"

"Yeah. Go up the stairs. It's a real nice apartment up there. Cool place to live, if you're not dead." As the window rolled up, she could hear the cops chuckling at their own humor. Ha ha, death scene joke. Never funny.

She paused in the biting wind to pull on shoe covers and gloves, then pushed into the building. The door slammed shut with a bang behind her as she stared at the image of a blood-spattered girl. It was a movie poster for the horror film *Carrie,* a splash of Technicolor gore that would surely startle every visitor who walked in the door. Hanging on the exposed redbrick walls of the entrance hall was a gallery of other movie posters, and as she climbed the stairs, she passed *Day of the Triffids, Pit and the Pendulum,* and *Night of the Living Dead.*

"Thought I heard the slam shut," Jane Rizzoli called down from the second-floor landing. She gestured to the movie posters. "Imagine coming home to those every night."

"These posters all look original. They're probably quite valuable."

"Talk about valuable, wait till you see this place."

Maura followed Jane into the apartment and paused to admire the massive oak beams and trendy brick walls. Renovations had transformed what was once a warehouse into a stunning loft that no starving artist could ever afford.

"Not bad, huh?" said Jane. "I could live here. Except for that creepy thing hanging on the wall." She pointed to a monstrous red eye that stared from a movie poster. "Notice the name of the movie?"

"*I See You,*" said Maura.

"Remember that title. It might be significant," Jane said ominously. She led Maura past an open kitchen with black granite countertops. The floor still had its original wide oak planks, now polished to a high gloss. "He found her in the bedroom."

"Who did?"

"Victim's father. He owns this building, lets her stay in the apartment. She lives alone here, no current boyfriend. She was supposed to meet Dad for lunch at a restaurant, and when she didn't show up, Dad drove here to check on her. Says he found the door unlocked, but the place otherwise looked fine to him. Until he got to the bedroom." Jane paused. "And that's all he was able to tell us before we had to call the ambulance."

"The cop downstairs told me it looked like he had a heart attack."

"Yeah. I thought I was going to have to do CPR."

Jane looked at the bedroom doorway. "No wonder. After what he saw in there."

Detective Barry Frost stood in the far corner of the bedroom, jotting in a notebook. His wintry pallor was even more pronounced than usual, and he managed only a feeble nod as Maura entered. She gave Frost scarcely a glance; her attention was fixed on the victim. The young woman lay in a strangely serene pose, arms at her side, as if she'd simply settled on top of the bedspread, fully dressed, for a nap. She was dressed all in black, in leggings and a turtleneck, emphasizing the ghostly whiteness of her face. Her hair was jet-black as well, but her blond roots betrayed the fact this was a dye job. Multiple gold studs pierced her ears, and a gold hoop gleamed on her right eyebrow. But it was what gaped beneath the eyebrows that drew Maura's shocked attention.

Both eye sockets were empty.

In horror, Maura looked down at the woman's left hand. At what was nestled like two dull marbles in her open palm.

"And *that's* what makes this a fun night, boys and girls," Jane said.

"Bilateral globe enucleation," said Maura softly.

"Is that fancy medical talk for *cutting out the eyeballs*?"

"Yes."

"I like how you give everything a dry clinical spin. It makes the fact she's holding her own eyeballs somehow seem less, oh, totally fucked up."

"Tell me about this victim," said Maura.

Frost looked up from his notebook. "Jenny

Coyle, twenty-six years old, lives—lived here—alone. She's an independent filmmaker, works out of a studio on South Street."

"Which Dad also owns," added Jane.

"What kind of films did she make?" asked Maura, although the answer already seemed obvious.

"Horror flicks."

"Which goes along with her sense of fashion," said Jane, eyeing the victim's pierced eyebrow and dyed black hair. "I thought goth was out of style, but she looks like she totally rocked it."

Reluctantly Maura focused on what was cradled in the victim's hand. Exposure to air had dried the corneas, and blue eyes that had once glistened while alive were now clouded. The ligamentous attachments were shriveled to brown nubbins, but she could still identify the intricate ocular muscles that so precisely controlled movements of the human eye.

"I sure as hell hope that operation was done postmortem," said Jane.

"It was. Judging by the palpebra."

"The what?"

"The eyelids. Do you see how there's no extraneous damage to the tissues?

Whoever did this took his time. That would be impossible if she were conscious and struggling. And there's minimal blood loss, which indicates her circulation was already shut down when the cutting began." Maura leaned closer. "The symbolism is fascinating."

Jane looked at Frost. "I told you she'd say that."

"The eyes are said to be the windows of the soul. Maybe the killer didn't like what he saw, or didn't like the way she looked at him. Maybe he felt threatened."

"Or maybe her movie had something to do with it," said Frost. *"I See You."*

Maura looked at him. "She made that movie?"

"*I See You* was her very first feature film, released two years ago. According to her dad, it was a flop that went straight to DVD. You never know which weirdo might have seen it."

"And been inspired by it," said Maura, staring down at Jenny Coyle's empty eye sockets. She grasped the right arm and tried to flex the elbow. The joint was immovable. "She's in full rigor mortis. When was she last seen alive?"

"Her dad said he spoke to her on the phone yesterday afternoon around four, while she was at work. We haven't interviewed her colleagues yet. We're hoping that security camera down the street caught something. Or someone."

Maura pulled up the hem of the victim's black turtleneck, exposing a telltale purplish discoloration that had pooled on the back. She pressed a gloved finger against the flesh. "Livor mortis appears fixed."

"So what do you think about time of death?"

"Twelve to twenty-four hours. I can't be more specific than that." She peeled down the turtleneck collar and examined the neck. "No ligature marks. No obvious trauma anywhere."

"Except for the eyeballs," said Jane. "He cuts out her eyeballs but doesn't take them as souvenirs.

Why place them in her hand? What the hell does it mean?"

"That's a question for a psychologist." With a sigh, Maura straightened. "I can't determine cause of death here. I need to examine her in the morgue."

"Overdose?" suggested Frost.

"The tox screen will give us the answer." Maura stripped off her gloves. "She'll be first on my autopsy schedule tomorrow. I'll see you there."

Maura left the bedroom and was walking out of the apartment when Jane said: "Before you go, can I ask you something?"

"Of course."

They stepped out onto the second floor landing and Jane shut the door behind them. "What's going on?" she asked quietly.

"I'm not sure what you're asking."

"You were in Framingham. You went to see Amalthea, didn't you?"

Calmly Maura buttoned up her coat. "You make it sound like I've committed a crime."

"Maybe not a crime. But it sure isn't very smart."

"She's in the ICU, Jane. I'm her only living relative, and she wanted to see me."

"She's using you. Playing on your sympathy."

"We'll talk about this some other time." Without a backward glance, Maura walked down the stairs and stepped outside. A frigid wind funneled down the street, lashing her hair and face.

Jane followed her outside and as Maura walked down Utica Street, Jane was right behind her. "What does she want?"

"She's dying of cancer. What do you think she wants?"

"To mess with your head. She knows how to twist people, Maura. Look what she did to your brother. Look how *he* ended up."

"You think I'd ever be like—"

"Of course not! But you said it yourself once. You said you were born with the same streak of darkness. She'll use it against you."

"This is my business, Jane." She unlocked her Lexus and slid inside. "*My* decision."

"Okay, okay." Jane held up both hands. "But don't say I didn't warn you."

Through the car window, Maura watched Jane stride away, back to the crime scene. Back to the room where a dead woman lay in bed, body frozen in rigor mortis. A woman with no eyes.

Amalthea's words suddenly came back to her: *They'll find another one soon.*

She locked the car doors and quickly scanned the street, the buildings. Did something just move in that dark alleyway? Why did the couple in the sandwich shop seem to be watching her? Everywhere she looked, she saw ominous silhouettes. This was what Jane had warned her about. This was Amalthea's power; she'd opened a curtain and revealed a nightmarish landscape where nothing was as it appeared, and everything was painted in shadow.

Maura started the car and icy air blasted from the heater vent. It's time to go home, she thought. To the light.